The Summer of Shambles

EBONY MCKENNA

The decision to leave a career in journalism was a logical choice for Ebony. There wasn't enough time in the day to write the fictional stories she wanted to tell, against the factual that she had to tell. She followed her heart towards writing science fiction, romance and young adult adventures. Ebony now writes full time and lives in Melbourne, Australia, with her husband and young son. She loves trivia nights, train sets and the Eurovision Song Contest.

www.ebonymckenna.com

ONDINE

The Summer of Shambles

EBONY McKENNA

EGMONT

EGMONT
We bring stories to life

Ondine: The Summer of Shambles first published in Great Britain 2010
by Egmont UK Limited
239 Kensington High Street
London W8 6SA

Text copyright © Ebony McKenna 2010
Cover photograph: Dimitri Vervitsiotis
Photographer's Choice RF/Getty Images

The moral rights of the author and cover illustrator have been asserted

ISBN 978 1 4052 4961 4

1 3 5 7 9 10 8 6 4 2

A CIP catalogue record for this title is available
from the British Library

Typeset by Avon DataSet Ltd, Bidford on Avon, Warwickshire

Printed and bound in Great Britain by the CPI Group

Dedicated to the memory of Frank Muir,
a true gentleman and kind mentor.

BRUGEL (pron. Broo-gl) Officially **The Serene Duchy of Brugel.** Brugel is a small country in eastern Europe. It has a single house of parliament, called 'the Dentate' (the place with teeth). The First Minister is the head of government. The Duke of Brugel is the head of state.

Brugel is at the crossroads of old and new Europe. Previously part of the USSR, Brugel declared independence in 1991 and shares its borders with Slaegal to the north and east, Craviç to west and the Black Sea to the south. The capital and largest city is Venzelemma. The Brugel language is derived from an earlier form of English. This came about after many Jutes, Angles and Saxons took a wrong turn in the fifth century and found themselves at the Black Sea.

Brugel has survived through many hardships, having been annexed into the Constantine, Austro-Hungarian, Prussian and Holy Roman empires at various – and mercifully short – times in history. In the 1950s Soviet tanks often rumbled through the main streets of Venzelemma – on their way to somewhere else.

Any rumours you may have heard about Brugel are probably true. All psychics and mediums can trace their DNA to the foothills of Brugel. The countryside is the birthplace of gypsy folklore, and fairy tales and talking animals are interwoven in daily life. This is a country where the strange and unusual are not only tolerated, they are encouraged.

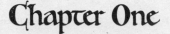

Chapter One

This is a great story, and like a good many great stories before it, it begins with a teenage girl. Her name is Ondine de Groot and she is fifteen. She has long dark hair past her shoulders, which is neat for about five minutes before it gets messy and stringy. Her eyes are dark brown and pretty, except when she's rolling them. She also adores small animals, of which you will hear more in a moment.

Ondine's story begins exactly twelve years ago today, in a place called Brugel,[1] a pretty country in eastern Europe which is well known for its old

---

1 *One of the former Eastern Bloc countries. Brugel is mostly famous for three things. It has the only hexagonal flag in the world. Its main export is plütz, a tasty yet highly volatile vodka made from peaches. It has also never won the Eurovision Song Contest.*

buildings.[2] On the day this story begins, Ondine was nearing the end of her time at Psychic Summercamp. As the name suggests, Psychic Summercamp is a place for students to spend their holidays developing their psychic and other extra-sensory skills. In some countries, students spend their holidays at adventure camp, fat camp or mathletics. In Brugel, they do things differently.

Back to Ondine. She is in a dormitory with three other girls (who are asleep on account of it being so early in the morning) and she's just woken with a jolt.

'Saturn's rings! It's six o'clock! I've slept through the astral projection exam.' Ondine sat up and pushed the covers away. The bed's throw fell to the floor, smothering the furry black ferret that lay curled up on a patch of rug beneath.

'Melody, wake up,' she said, nudging the sleeping girl in the bunk above her. 'What happened in the astral exam?'

---

2   *From a strategic point of view, Brugel was so insignificant during World War Two that neither the Allies nor the Axis bothered to bomb it. This is why so many of its old buildings are still standing.*

It took Melody a few more nudges to wake up. Yawning, she swiped her mousy-blonde hair from her face, rubbed the sleep from her eyes and inspected it, then stopped as she realised she had an audience.

'Ah, sorry.' Melody looked embarrassed as she blinked herself awake. 'What's going on, what time is it? The sun isn't even up.' The psychic lessons didn't seem to have worked very well on her either.

'Shh, you'll wake the others,' Ondine said. 'Now, quick, what happened in the astral?'

'I . . . I don't know. I must have slept through it!' Melody's face crumpled and she made ready to cry. 'I'm going to fail, aren't I?'

'Don't worry, I'll fail more than you.' As Ondine looked around the room, she spotted the handle of her suitcase poking out from under her bed. It gave her an idea. 'This entire thing is a waste of time, and a waste of our summer holidays. I'm going to run away to home.'

A great many girls of Ondine's age would love to run away *from* home, but Ondine was the other way around. She'd had it up to here (hold your hand at eyebrow level) with the whole psychic thing and knew it was time to quit.

While Melody watched the door for teachers, Ondine packed up her clothes and her gimgaws[3] and doohickie whatsits and zipped the case closed.

'Shouldn't you tell Mrs Howser you're leaving?' Melody asked.

'Pfft. She's the psychic one, why should I bother?' Ondine looked at the sleeping forms of her remaining roommates. 'You can tell the other two when they wake up.'

'How will you get home?' Melody asked.

Valid question. Psychic Summercamp was located on the outskirts of Brugel's capital city, Venzelemma, and Ondine's family lived right over on the other side.

'There's a bus stop down the end of the street, so I'll take that to central station. Then I'll get the train the rest of the way home.' Ondine sounded rather pleased with her plan as she lifted the throw off the ferret and folded it into a messy rectangle-ish shape on

---

3 *This was during the enormous gimgaw craze, so everyone had them. You won't find them now though.*

4

the end of her bed. The throw, not the animal. Ferrets don't fold so well.

'What about Shambles?' Melody asked, looking at the sleeping animal on the ground.

Oh dear. Ondine hadn't given much thought to the ferret, because she didn't think the creature should be coming with her. Ondine was more your fluffy kitten-y type of girl, so she hadn't given much attention this morning to the long and skinny bundle of black. Turning up at home, unannounced, before Summercamp finished would give her family enough of a fright. Turning up unannounced with a weasel in her hands might finish her mother right off.

'He's a sweet thing, and he's really taken to you.' Melody's eyes were bright with possibilities.

'You're right,' Ondine agreed.

During the weeks at camp, Ondine and Shambles the ferret had become unlikely buddies. He'd turned up one day[4] and made himself at home, following Ondine about. He'd even come to classes with her. The

---

4 *She'd found him face-deep in her secret stash of Brugelwürst sausage, a local delicacy.*

thought of abandoning the little fella to the craziness of Summercamp and Mrs Howser made something twist in her tummy. Probably guilt. A bit of hunger too.

Then Shambles the ferret woke up, spun around a few times and stood up on his hind legs, looking like an elongated, begging puppy. If puppies had pointy noses, long whiskers and sharp teeth.

'And nobody else got a pet while they were here,' Melody said. 'You were really lucky.'

Hmmm, what to do? It wouldn't be right to leave him here.

'I'll take him with me and find him a good home,' Ondine said, scooping up the creature and tucking him into the crook of her arm. 'Shambles, you're going to have to behave yourself or I'll leave you on the bus.' It was her way of trying to sound stroppy. The little fella was pretty cute once you got to know him.

And that's how Ondine came to leave Psychic Summercamp on that warm summer's morning, with a ferret wrapped around her neck like a scarf and the scent of geraniums and lavender in her nostrils as she walked along the flower-studded footpath to the bus stop. The wind blew her hair in wild directions, whipping at her lips and eyes. There was nothing she could do to prevent it; she needed both hands to carry her heavy case. Not even a spare hand for Shambles – he hung on to her collar.

It wasn't until Ondine got off the bus and reached Venzelemma's crowded central train station that the ferret spoke.

'Thank gooniss for tha–, I'm all bumpy and broke,' Shambles said with a deep Scottish accent, then climbed on to her head to get a better view. 'Progress! The train'll be here in a minute. When we get tae yer hoose we can eet, I'm fair starven.'

Ondine gasped and dropped her case on the platform in shock. Because, make no mistake about it, there was definitely a man's voice coming from the ferret. Quickly, she found a place to sit down, then she hauled Shambles into her hands to have a good look at him, all the time wondering if she'd gone a bit . . . funny.

'I've lost my mind,' Ondine said. A furtive look around told her nobody else was paying them any attention. The station was full of grey-looking people heading off to work for the day, completely unaware of the teenage girl with scruffy brown hair holding a black ferret.

'Nae ye havnae, but ye can hear me,' Shambles added in his thick brogue. 'Looks like somethin' must hae rubbed off at Summercamp.'

Ondine rolled her eyes. 'Ma will be so pleased. All that gypsy blood in my veins and all I can do is talk to rodents.'

'I'm nae rodent, ye bampot,[5] I'm a ferret. Completely different. Right then, hae comes the loco. Let me at yer neck.'

'But . . . but!' Ondine's brain turned to slurry as she tried to make sense of this talking animal. All the while heated embarrassment roared up her neck and face.

'No backing out now, lassie. I'm coming with ye. Now grab the case and on we get. And upon my honour, I promise to behave.'

What could she do? It was still such a shock that

---

5 *Silly person. Daftie. Gets low grades at school and later in life rarely earns more than minimum wage.*

her new furry friend could talk. And why could she only hear him now? At that moment the train[6] pulled in and Ondine had no more time for prevaricating.

It was a tense ride home on the train, what with the uncomfortable wooden seats, a talking ferret wriggling about her neck and passengers giving her very strange looks. As soon as the engine arrived at her home station, Ondine grabbed Shambles away from her throat and put him on her shoulder.

His little paws reached up to the top of her head. He stretched and had a good look around.

'Oh, so ye live in *this* part of town, how very la-de-dah! No wonder yer parents have money tae pish away on psychic dafties.'

By this point you may have formed the opinion that Shambles was not your run-of-the-mill ferret, and you'd be right. You may have also formed the opinion

---

6 *Venzelemma is home to one of the oldest elektrichka train fleets in Europe. Their sparse interiors and spine-jarringly uncomfortable wooden bench seats evoke equal amounts of old world nostalgia and sciatica. Most chiropractors in Brugel are located within hobbling distance of train stations.*

that he's saucy and cheeky, and you'd be right there too. But if you think he's nothing but trouble, you're wrong, although he does give that impression.

As keen as she was to race home, Ondine waited for the train to clear the station before she stepped off the end of the platform to walk across the tracks, looking both ways to make sure no other trains were coming. The pedestrian overpass would have been safer, but it was closed to the public until the official opening.

'Pinch me, I'm dreaming,' Shambles said as he noted the direction Ondine was taking him. 'The girl lives in a pub!'

The ferret spoke the truth. Ondine's parents ran a hotel and public bar on the main road in a pretty swanky part of Venzelemma. Three storeys tall and painted bright blue and white, the hotel towered over the neighbourhood. As neighbourhoods go, the de Groots' part of Venzelemma was one of the nicer ones, with a good mix of residences and businesses, and far removed from the fish markets. Even the newer buildings looked like old buildings to help them blend in.

The Station Hotel prided itself on being a family

business, where everyone pitched in and helped. Not yet old enough to serve alcohol in the bar, Ondine worked in the dining room and helped out behind the scenes. A lot.

Most people think if your parents run a restaurant, you eat delicious five-course meals every night.

You don't.

Ask anyone what it's really like and they'll tell you it's nothing but work. Washing dishes, ironing tablecloths, cleaning the floors, chopping wood for the fire, keeping the fire going all night, preparing food. Look, the list just goes on and on.

But for Ondine, working at home with her parents appealed more than howling at the moon or looking for omens in tea leaves or reading palms or any other great wastes of time that sucked away her precious summer holidays.

'Wait up, we cannae just walk in. Yer mother will fair faint,' Shambles said, holding on to Ondine's shoulder.

That made Ondine stop for a moment and think about her plan of action.

'She'll be glad to see me,' she said. 'Although I don't know what she'll make of you. She's not the pet kind.'

'I'm nobody's pet!' Shambles clenched his paws on his hips in frustration. 'And dinnae tell no one about finding a new home for me. Yer the first person who's heard me in scores of years, mebbe more. I've lost count. I need ye tae stick around and help me, because I think I'm losing my social skills.'[7]

Laughter caught in Ondine's throat. She dumped her suitcase on the ground to catch her breath. It had been a trying morning to say the least, and she wasn't used to lugging heavy things for long distances. Plates piled high with food were fine, because they only needed carrying from the kitchen to the dining-room tables. Heavy suitcases were another matter entirely.

Picking up her suitcase with a grunt, Ondine resumed her walk to the back door. 'Are all ferrets like you? I mean, how come you can talk?'

'Because I'm *nawt* a real ferret. I'm a man. My name's Hamish McPhee, but I offended a witch and she turned me thus. I've bin like this for years. Powerful

---

7   *Pure denial. Shambles lost his social skills years ago.*

magic it was and all. Haven't a grey hair on me. Thank gooniss she used a staying spell.'

Ondine's eyes widened in surprise. 'You offended a witch? Wow!'

'Aye. She took it badly.'

'Obviously! You must have done something really awful to her.' Her mind reeled as she wondered what sort of offensive thing might make a witch turn a regular man into a weasel. A regular man! Ondine's memory leapt back to her time in Summercamp, when she'd allowed Shambles to sleep in her dorm. Well, that was before she'd known what he really was. Now that she did know, there'd be no more of that!

'Aye, and I'm deeply ashamed,' Shambles admitted.

'What did you do then? And is this witch about to descend on me and demand the return of her familiar?'[8] Had Ondine taken on more than she'd bargained for?

'I'm no *familiar!* They're silly animals turned into

---

8 *An animal form of supernatural spirit, who aids a witch in performing magic. Sometimes they're helpful, but in most cases they're useless. Have you ever seen a cat fetch the morning newspaper? Vacuum the floor? Make breakfast? Exactly.*

fat-belly pets. I'll have ye remember I'm a man living in reduced circumstances.'

'You're stalling. What did you do?'

'Aw, I was a right neep.[9] I was supposed tae partner her at a debutante ball. Ye know the ones, where the girls get all dolled up and look like brides? And then they get presented to some fancy-pants man, like a mayor or a duke.'

That gave Ondine cause for pause. 'It must have been a while ago. Hardly anyone does a deb any more. I know Ma was keen on us getting presented, but it's all a bit old-fashioned and silly.'

'Too right, that's what I thought. But this girl took it real serious-like. And I didnae. I wasnae yer ideal partner, on account of the fact I had ma first taste of plütz[10] that night.'

His tone of voice told Ondine he felt truly sorry for his actions, and she started to feel a bit sorry for him in return.

---

9 *Neep. Short for turnip.*

10 *Plütz is Brugel's number one alcoholic export. It is made from fermented peaches, is 32 per cent proof and is the main ingredient in divorce proceedings.*

By now they'd reached the back door. Ondine fished around in her pockets for her key and made ready to let them in. The smell of fried breakfast foods wafted from the kitchen windows, making her tummy rumble.

'Out with it then.'

'It's embarrassing –'

This ought to be good. 'I'm sure it is. Hurry up, I need breakfast.'

'Aw, breakfast. I could murder some big fatty sausage,' Shambles said, his tongue licking the fur around his mouth in anticipation.

'Stop stalling,' Ondine said, clenching her hands into fists by her sides. 'Tell me what happened, and then we'll have breakfast.'

'Ooooh, listen to ye! All grown up and sophisticated, like,' Shambles teased, then Ondine stared daggers at him and his voice dropped to a sombre tone. 'I didn't know she was a real witch, otherwise I wouldnae called her one. But she was getting snippy with me, so I ducked off and had some more plütz. It's like peaches and rocket fuel that stuff, and I've nawt touched it since. Then she got really pished with me when I stepped on her feet and fell over. I ripped the lacy bit at the bottom of her skirt and then she got really mad. She called me pond scum. I called her a witch. She looked like her head might explode. She said, "You're damn right I'm a witch. And you're nothing better than a low-down weasel," and then she said I could stay like that.'

'Wow. And she turned you into a ferret, right there in front of everyone?'

'Naw, she turned me into a donkey! Of *course* she turned me into a ferret! She was fair affronted.'

It took a few moments for Ondine to run the scenario through her head. 'But she called you a weasel, not a ferret. So how did that work?'

'I guess mebbe she didn't use the right words. Ferrets are smaller than weasels, but we're the same family, so maybe I am a low-down weasel after all. But between ye and me, I prefer ferret.'

A silence hung in the air, and then Ondine giggled. 'I think she did the right thing. Debutante balls take a lot of organising, and a lot of rehearsals. People take them very seriously. I think you should apologise to this poor girl as soon as possible. Then you might be yourself again.' The thought of Shambles becoming himself again made her wonder. What would he look like if he were real again? Maybe he wasn't much older than she was. As Shambles had said, the witch had used the right kind of spell to preserve his age, which set her mind to thinking all sorts of lovely possibilities. His voice alone made her grin.

Opening the back door, the pungent odour of fried meats and old beer greeted them.

'Aww, that's the good stuff.' Shambles took a huge and very noisy sniff.

'Ondine! What are you doing home?' her mother called out from the hallway.

'Hi, Ma, you look great. Have you lost weight? I love your hair.' Her mother looked as plump as ever, but her new burgundy-brown hairdo skimmed her face and made her look thinner. Flattery ought to put her in a good mood. Just to be on the safe side, Ondine adopted what she hoped was a pleading look on her face. 'I . . . I got homesick so I came back.'

Ma stopped mid-stride, mouth open, when she saw the ferret on her daughter's shoulder. 'Heavens above!

What is that?' She pointed to the ferret with one hand, while the other patted the ample bosom above her heart, as if the beating organ might leap from her chest.

It called for quick thinking on Ondine's part, because her mother could be either furious or happy about the situation. There was often no advance warning of which way the mood might take her.

'He's really tame. Please, Ma, let me keep him?'

But Shambles was having none of it. 'That's the one!' he cried out, finally finding his voice. He scurried down the back of Ondine's vest. 'That's the witch!'

Chapter Two

'I am not a witch,' her mother said. 'Ondine, is there a man just out the back door? With a Scottish accent?'

A sick little feeling settled in Ondine's stomach as she took in her mother's pale, shocked face. 'You heard him?'

'Yes, I did hear him, and he called me a witch.' Then the crease in Ma's forehead relaxed and the tension in her shoulders fell away. 'And, by the way, it's lovely to see you.' She moved forwards to embrace her daughter. Around her neck she wore three gold rings with rubies set in them. They flashed in the light as they bounced and jiggled. Just as Ondine thought they might hug, her mother's shoulders hitched again and her eyebrows shot up. She must have seen the ferret hanging off her daughter's back.

'Ondi, I didn't expect you back so soon, but you can tell me why later. We're run off our feet – I could use another pair of hands. Good thing school doesn't start back for a few weeks yet otherwise I'd be in real strife. You can fill me in on Summercamp later. Right now I need you to tell me what that ferret is doing on your back.'[11]

'OK, Shambles, the jig is up, off you get.' It wasn't easy, but Ondine contorted her body and pulled the reluctant critter away from the middle of her back. 'Ma, meet Shambles. Shambles, this is my mother, Colette.'

'Naw, lass, hide me!'

'What?' Ondine exclaimed.

'Run for yer life!'

'Stop wriggling, Shambles! What on earth's wrong with you? You just called my mother a witch, so you'd better apologise now or it's the gutter for you!' So

---

11 *In case you're wondering, Ondine's mother was very good at doing several things at once, so she talked like that too. On a good day she could get five or even seven subjects into a single sentence.*

much had happened in such a short time, Ondine felt
sure she must be running on pure adrenalin.

It was left to Ma to break the tension. 'Bless my
soul, a talking ferret! Ondine, is this your familiar? Is
this what you've brought back from your studies?'

Ondine explained the true situation. Ma laughed
loud and hearty, making the rings around her neck
jiggle and jump.

'I know who you are, Shambles,' she continued.
'You're that weasel what slighted my auntie and ruined
her presentation! Hamish McPhee, the Laird of Glen
Logan.'

Stunned amazement turned Ondine mute for a
second.

Shambles piped up, 'The witch who turned me is
yer *auntie*? Nawt ye? But if yer all wrinkly, she must be
double-wrinkly . . . or dead, no?'

'You're well suited to being a ferret, Shambles.'
Colette wiped tears of mirth from her eyes. 'My auntie
Col is eighty-five years young and in perfect health, I'll
have you know.'

It was a case of mistaken identity, on account of

the fact that Ondine's mother bore such a striking resemblance to Ondine's great-aunt. They both had the same short stature, plump faces that smiled a lot, deep brown eyes and dark hair. Ondine too had inherited most of those features, except she was already taller than her mother (or perhaps Ma had started shrinking?). The fact that Ondine's ma and great-aunt had the same first name only added to the confusion.

'Aw naw, aw naw! I've lawst tha will tae live,' Shambles bellowed. 'If she's eighty-five, what does that make me? I must hae been a ferret half a century then!'

'You're old enough to know better, even if you haven't aged in ferret form. You're the same age now as you were when you were turned.' Colette picked up Ondine's case and lugged it towards their family quarters. 'My auntie warned me about boys like you, and she was right, you'll never learn. You're lucky you're still a ferret, otherwise I wouldn't let you near my daughters. Given your taste for the sauce, I shouldn't let you anywhere near the bar either.'

Yikes! Better not tell Ma about how much time he spent in my room at Summercamp, otherwise I'll never hear the end of it.

Another thought flickered through her head – *A laird, eh? I wonder what lairds look like?*

'So, can we keep him?' Ondine asked her ma. 'I mean, it wouldn't be fair if we set him out on the street. He can sleep in the laundry. I'll make him a bed in there.'

'Are you a good mouser?' Ma asked, as she gave Shambles a serious looking over.

'Sure, why d'ye ask? Have ye a wee gun and holster for me?'

'You'll keep,' Ma said with one arched brow, then steered them towards the stairs. 'Sorry, Ondi, we're full up and I've had to rent out your room on account that I didn't think you'd be back for another fortnight. You can share with Cybelle for now.'

'Oh, Ma, not again,' Ondine said, unable to stop the whine in her voice. 'Cybelle snores.'

'And I'm sure she'll be delighted to see you too. Come down for breakfast and bring Hamish the Shambles with you when you're done. We'll have a family meeting to remember.'

When Ma was out of earshot, Shambles whispered,

'Why does she wear those rings around her neck?'

A dry grin crept over Ondine's face. 'It's because she's working with food all day – it's not hygienic.' The absolute truth? Her mother, having borne three children, had grown too big for her baubles.

What Ma promised, she delivered. The entire family squeezed around the breakfast table, watching Shambles snaffle sausage after sausage. All the while he made lickety-sloppity-chompity noises as he ate.

'He's so ugly! He looks like a strung-out rat,' said Marguerite, the eldest at twenty-one and a quarter. Marguerite would know about ugly, being so far removed from it herself. She had inherited the best of her parents' looks. Deep brown eyes framed with long lashes, tidy arched eyebrows, glossy brown hair that waved and curled in just the right way and always looked neat.

'But he has a . . .' Ondine nearly said 'lovely', but even she couldn't bring herself to say that. Instead she settled for, 'cute . . . personality.'

'The health inspector won't like it, not after we

had rats this winter,' Ondine's father, Josef, said. 'So you'd better keep him under wraps until you can find a new home for him.' Josef stood out amongst the sea of brunettes, having turned completely grey. His eyebrows, however, had not. They remained stubbornly black and threatened to join in the middle.

'But he's her assignment,' Ma said. 'He's Ondine's new familiar – it's all part of the programme. He has to stay otherwise she'll fail the course.'

Those comments – otherwise known as outright fibs – made Ondine's jaw fall open in shock, before she shut it in a hurry. If Da knew Shambles was a real lad, close to Ondine's age, he would throw him out. Ma had also side-stepped the issue of Ondine quitting Summercamp two weeks early.

Da was annoyed. 'I paid good money for that place, and they send them home as part of it? I want a refund.'

'I'll look into it,' Ma said in her most soothing tone.

'Go along with it. I'll nawt protest,' Shambles whispered between mouthfuls.

The sight of wet food chunks falling out of

Shambles's gob on to the table provided Ondine with an idea. She shovelled the meal into her mouth, to prevent having to talk or answer questions with anything more than a nod or shake of the head, lest she spray her family. If Ma did all the talking, Ondine didn't have to tell any lies . . . as such.

The middle daughter, Cybelle, who was nineteen, added to the fray. 'He can sit on the piano while I play in the evenings. He can guard the tips jar with those nippy little fangs of his.' As a performer, Cybelle also kept herself very neat. She was lucky enough to have dead-straight hair, cut in a bob with a thick fringe.

If Ondine hadn't had a mouth full of food, she would have told Cybelle she liked her new eyeliner, and could she borrow it please.

'Excellent, that settles it.' Ma looked happy with herself. 'OK, meeting's over, we all have work to do. Ondi, you and Belle are on laundry duty, Margi's in the kitchen with me on food prep, Josef, check the bar supplies. The Plütz Appreciation Society is coming to lunch.'

The PAS was a band of men and women dedicated

to damaging their stomachs, livers and kidneys in the most pleasurable way possible. They arrived as ladies and gentlemen and left as purple-lipped human debris, leaving an enormous mess behind them. However, they also left the hotel a sizeable pile of cash for their troubles, so they were always welcome to return.

'I'd better get a stiff broom too, so we can sweep them out before the dinner crowd turn up,' Josef said, rising from the table. As he passed Ondine, he paused and kissed the top of her head. 'It's lovely to have you back.'

'So, ye cannae hear me then?' Shambles said to the man of the house, making Ondine hold her breath for the answer. But no answer came.

How odd that her mother could hear him, but not her father. Perhaps only women could hear Shambles – or maybe only relatives of Aunt Col? In that case, why hadn't Cybelle or Marguerite heard him either?

That's the trouble with ferrets. Just when you thought you had them figured out, they managed to surprise you.

* * *

After checking out his new digs in the laundry, Shambles had no intention of catching mice or rats or anything else that might bite him back. Instead, he spent the late afternoon hanging around the kitchen door, catching food scraps Ma and Ondine threw his way.

He was in a pub, and that meant there was beer to be had. But how? The family wouldn't let him near the ale taps and he couldn't very well sit in full view of the public, because – he remembered with a shudder – drunks loved to shove him down their trousers.

Ditching Cybelle's plans to sit him on the top of the piano in the dining room, he slunk through the shadows into the front bar. The noise hit him like a wall, with every table full, and everyone talking at once. In the far corner, people played darts and shouted out their scores. The scent of hops and barley filled his senses, making him feel light-headed. In places, the carpet was so sticky he had to wrench his paws just to keep moving. Another problem was avoiding clumping great human feet.

He hid under a table in the darkened far corner. It wasn't so noisy over here. Three men sat hunched over their frothy drinks. One squeezed lemon juice over a bowl of hot chips, then shook pepper over them. The powder went everywhere, falling like grey snow over Shambles's head, making his eyes water. It was a warm night, and he envied how people could take their jackets off to cool down. Being stuck with a fur coat, he didn't have that option. Instead, he licked his legs to cool down. The air felt so thick and humid, he could almost taste the beer with each grooming lick, along with plenty of ground pepper. Yet all he achieved was wet fur. There had to be a better way to cool down. A plan took shape in his head. When the drinkers at the table above him went to the bathroom, he'd dash up on to the table and help himself to their dregs. A nice drink would hit the spot.

Only, it didn't quite go to plan, because what the men talked about at that table made his insides scrunch up. The more Shambles heard, the more he wanted to crawl up the closest trouser leg and sink his fangs into soft flesh. That would teach them a lesson. But the longer he delayed any course of action, the more he heard, and it was damning stuff.

Which only made him want to hear more.

When the men did eventually get up, he saw their scuffed boots heading towards the front door. There was nothing for it, he had to follow.

It was good to be home, despite the work – or maybe because of it. Ondine loved feeling useful, and she felt very useful in the kitchen, helping make meals, taking food to tables and sharing jokes with the patrons. The more she smiled, the bigger the tips. Even the mean ones could usually come around – and if they didn't, no harm done, they'd be gone in a few hours.

Tonight, the dining room resounded with chatter and music, with Cybelle on piano taking requests and Marguerite in the bar pouring the beers with Josef. Their father kept track of the money and also made sure the tipsy patrons kept their hands off his daughters. With her shiny hair, previously mentioned deep brown eyes and not-previously-mentioned Cupid's bow lips, Marguerite was the looker of the family. Exactly why Josef kept her closest to him.

'It's not his fault he's so uptight,' Ma said to Ondine in the kitchen.

'How did you know what I was thinking?' Sometimes she'd swear her mother was the psychic one. Maybe Ma should have gone to Summercamp instead.

'He thinks all men are lecherous drunks, but he can't help it because they are what he mostly sees. I try and tell him there are some good ones out there, that he's not the only decent man left in Brugel. But it's falling on deaf ears. Right, here are the meals for table eleven, out you get.'

Many people would find the truncated and many-threaded conversations confusing but Ondine was used to them. She made her way to the table and placed the food down.

Across the dining room, a woman screamed.

'Aaaaaaaaahhhh! A rat!'

Not again! Ondine's heart sank for a moment at the thought of rodents infiltrating the rooms. Just as quickly, her spirits lifted when she saw the blur of long black fur.

'It's all right, everyone relax. It's just my pet ferret,'

she said, scooping Shambles off the floor and on to her shoulder. She stroked the top of his smooth head. 'He's very clean and harmless. I apologise for the disruption.'

Time to get away before things got out of hand. How stupid of Shambles to be scurrying around the dining room! They'd be sure to get another visit from the health inspector after this.

'You are in so much trouble, Mister!' Ondine hissed as they made for the family's private room on the other side of the kitchen.

'Hear me out, lass, there's *merdah* afoot and I came tae warn ye. I heard them plotting the whole thing. I followed one of them, man's got a head like a guiser's neep.[12] We have tae warn the Duke.'

'What's going on?' The voice belonged to Ma, who'd heard the commotion and followed them out to the back room. 'Why was Shambles running around the dining room?'

---

12 *Incredibly ugly person, with reference to the hollowed-out turnips with candles in them, used on Guy Fawkes Night. Imagine someone with a face like a turnip that's probably been smashed in a few times. And then run over.*

'I think he heard people plotting to kill someone.'

'Aye, I did! They were in the front bar, drinking their courage and plotting their evil against the Duke of Brugel. I know where they live. We have tae take action, before it's too late.'

Ma threw her hands skywards. 'I can't just abandon a full house!'

'But Ma, someone's going to get killed!' Ondine said.

'OK, OK. If what you say is true, Shambles, then you're right, the Duke needs to be warned. Ondine, I'll get your da and the two of you can warn him.'

'The three of us,' Shambles corrected.

'What do you mean the three of us? I can't leave, we're only halfway through dinner,' Ma said.

'Naw. I mean *I'm* goin' with Ondi and Josef. I'll tell them everything I heard as we go – it will save time,' Shambles said.

'But what do we tell him?' Ondine asked. 'How do we explain to royalty that a ferret told us about a murder plot?'

'We'll tell him you overheard the plot, Ondi, while you were tending tables in the bar,' Shambles instructed.

'But . . . but . . .' Confusion bubbled in her veins and sapped her brain. Never in her life had she felt so out of control, and that was saying something for a girl with two older sisters who lived in a pub.

'Hurry lass, there's no time to lose. Do you want the Duke's blood on your hands?'

Chapter Three

ow they reached the Duke of Brugel's city domain that night isn't important, but what they said to him when they got there is, so we'll pick up the story from there.[13]

'It's so big,' Ondine said as they approached the gates of the Duke's domain.

Big didn't even come close. Humongous would be more apt.[14] Ondine let Josef do all the talking at the security gate, then a sentry walked them across the vast gravel expanse towards the side entry. The looming walls and dark shadows sucked all the

---

13 *It should be noted that you can't just rock up to the Duke of Brugel's city estate and say hello. He's a very busy man. He has a whole country to run. In this case, because of the seriousness of Ondine and her da's claims, the Duke decided to make an exception.*

14 *The Duke's city residence is so big it has its own postcode.*

warmth from the summer's evening.

Ondine's breath came in short bursts and her feet ached. As they walked along the cavernous hallway, the echoes of their footsteps reverberated in her ears. No ordinary tiles on this floor. She marvelled at the intricate mosaic work and wondered how many years it had taken to make it. A cool chill settled in her neck, despite Shambles wrapping himself around her like a stole. For his part, Shambles remained as still as it was possible for a ferret to remain still, so the Duke wouldn't notice how alive he was.

They entered a large room and waited. The Duke cast an imposing figure as he arrived, dressed in a suit and tie, and took a seat at the other end of the room. Standing so far away from him, Ondine felt small and insignificant. The sentry put his hand out to let them know they were not allowed to step any closer.

From the distance, Ondine could see very little of the Duke, except his silvery white hair, which curled back in soft waves from a pronounced widow's peak. He had the classic Brugel split moustache, which is shaved at the philtrum,[15] and a narrow goatee, which he stroked thoughtfully.

'My Lord Duke,' Josef began with a steady and loud voice. He bowed his head and very nearly tugged at a forelock of hair while he was at it.

Ondine was impressed that her father knew the correct way to address a duke. But then Da loved his tradition, so perhaps it wasn't so surprising.

'We apologise for the late hour and the interruption to your family, but time is against us. My name is Josef de Groot and my family owns the Station Hotel. Our clientele is well behaved and law-abiding, but tonight my daughter, Ondine, overheard people in our public bar plotting to do harm to your person. We came as quickly as we could. To warn you.'

'Really?' The Duke's voice carried across the room. It was hard to tell from the distance, but he didn't seem that interested. He stroked his goatee again. 'And why should I take your word for it? How do I know you're

15 *The philtrum is the cute little indent just below your nose. It is also the trickiest part to shave and requires a steady hand and very narrow razor.*

not just scamming for money? You could be part of the plot, looking to be paid off.'

'Yes, Your Grace, all good points. Your criticism does you credit. Perhaps my daughter could explain,' Josef said, giving Ondine a nudge of encouragement.

From behind her ear, she heard Shambles's reassuring whisper, 'Tell him what I told you about the plot, that they plan tae do him in at the railway station tomorrow morning, at the opening of the new overpass.'

So Ondine did, trying to make her voice loud enough to be heard but not shouting, which would be rude.

Then Shambles gave Ondine a detailed description of the men's faces, and told her to tell that to the Duke as well.

'One of them was also missing the top half of his index finger,' Ondine relayed with due diligence.

'Aye, probably picking his nose when someone punched him in the face,' Shambles whispered.

That bit did not bear repeating. Ondine needed all her strength to bite her tongue and stop the bubbling laugh in her throat from escaping. It didn't take Psychic Summercamp lessons to know the Duke would not appreciate comedy at this point. Not when people wanted to kill him in the morning. With an audience and everything.

'Hmm,' the Duke said after thinking some more. 'Step closer.'

The sentry allowed them to take six paces before stopping them once again. They were closer, but far from intimate.

'You came upon this plot how?' the Duke asked.

Ondine repeated everything Shambles told her. 'I was serving a table nearby, and overheard some of their conversation. I came back and cleared another table so I could keep listening.'

For a while the Duke stopped stroking his goatee and pondered the information, as was his right. He'd just been delivered a huge shock. He was entitled to paranoia. This time somebody really was out to get him. He was well within his rights to pause and think.

After a few more moments of thought, in which Ondine shifted her weight from her left leg to her right and back again, the Duke motioned to the sentry to let them get even closer. Another six steps. They were about three metres apart.

'How old are you, child?'

'*Say you're eighteen, say you're eighteen,*' Shambles whispered furiously from behind her ear. The ferret was smart to remind her, because if she told the truth, the Duke might ask questions about underage girls serving alcohol. A fifteen-year-old serving in a pub? Not good at all.

'I'm nineteen, Your Grace,' Ondine said, figuring if she had to lie, she might as well make it a good one. 'And I think I'd like to stay nineteen for a long while to come.'

A smile split the Duke's face. 'I understand. My dear wife has been thirty-four for many years now.'

Ondine dared not look at her father, in case he became confused and gave the game away. To his credit, he started making excuses about getting back to the hotel, lest the patrons take advantage of reduced staff numbers. The Duke had other ideas. He wanted more information, and it was clear from his expression that he wouldn't let them cross back over the threshold until he had it.

The sound of footsteps caught their attention. It came from the top of the curved timber staircase to their right. The conversation stopped.

An embarrassing heat crept up Ondine's neck and face as she looked at the handsome owner of the footsteps, with his tousled dark blond hair and deep brown eyes.

'Lord Vincent.' Josef gave a diplomatic nod of his head, while at the same time his hand reached towards Ondine's. 'We will not trouble your father a moment longer. Come along, Ondine, good girl.'

'On the contrary. You're no trouble,' the Duke said.

But Ondine's father had other concerns. Naturally, he'd know the name of the Duke's son – his paternal radar knew the identity of every bachelor in the immediate three counties. Despite what her mother had said earlier in her father's defence, Ondine found it really hard to see things through her da's eyes. OK, a lot of men were drunks, but not all the men who came to the pub got roaring drunk, and not every man in

41

the world spent time in pubs. Was he ever going to see things that way, or was he stuck in the Middle Ages?

Ondine wasn't looking at the master of the house any more, she could only look at the son, while her pulse started beating just that naughtily bit faster in her ears. He looked perhaps nineteen, maybe a little older, and his expression gave him an air of moneyed confidence. Like his father, he wore a suit and tie, but an updated version, the kind that looked effortlessly expensive. Lord Vincent descended the staircase and walked deliberately towards her, a smile playing at the edges of his mouth. All of which gave Ondine the chance to appreciate his features.

'Vincent, is there something you want, boy?' The Duke's voice sounded terse.

The young lord's buoyancy dimmed a fraction. Ondine could see an annoyed look cross his face.

A familiar pang took hold in Ondine. Despite their differences in social status, they shared something in common – parents who expected them to behave as adults, but treated them like children.

'No, sir,' Vincent said. In the blink of an eye he reset

his features, giving him fresh confidence as if nothing could trouble him. 'I was merely on my way out to an engagement.'

'Right then. Be home by two, and don't bring any flotsam back with you this time,' the Duke said.

A nod was all that the Duke received in return. As Vincent walked past Ondine towards the door, she dared a glance and saw him roll his eyes. An inappropriate giggle formed, but she tamped it down.

'I don't like him,' Shambles whispered.

If not for the Scottish accent, Ondine would have sworn the words had come straight from her father.

When the meeting with the Duke finally finished, Josef hustled them back to the hotel so they could resume work, all the while lecturing Ondine about the dangers of unruly boys.

'Don't fall for the first boy who pays you attention. Keep yourself nice,' he said as they approached the family pub.

'Da, give me a little credit, *please*, and stop treating me like a kid,' Ondine whined, betraying her maturity.

'That's right, you're *nineteen*, aren't you? Trying to act all sophisticated to impress the little lord.'

'I was not! I only lied about my age because the Duke asked how old I was, and if I'd told him the truth, then he'd wonder why an underage girl was serving alcohol. I was saving *your* skin.'

'Hold your tongue,' Josef said as they walked through the gate to the rear garden, 'we're home now. Time for you to get back to work.'

Just when Ondine thought she'd won the argument, Da had pulled the 'I'm your father' routine, using it like a get-out-of-jail-free card. His timing, as always, was perfect, because he usually called an end to their debates just as Ondine thought of some great comeback lines. Like, 'You were born old' and 'You're just grumpy because it saves time being anything else.' Words that would, for now, remain unspoken.[16] But before Ondine could work up a full head of steam, she saw something that took her breath away.

---

16 *Every time this happened, she promised herself she'd use these great lines next time she and her da had a barney. But it never worked out like that.*

It was a scene that made her appreciate her eldest sister more than cinnamon toast and marshmallows, because what they witnessed on that balmy summer evening made her father forget all about potential problems between Ondine and Lord Vincent.

There was her eldest sister Marguerite, in the darkened beer garden, all kissy-face with a young man.

'Margi, what is going on?' her father spluttered.

For a fleeting moment, Ondine felt sorry for her sister. In some respects, she could understand why her da ragged on to her about boys, because she was the youngest. But Margi was positively ancient and old enough to do whatever she liked in Ondine's eyes.

'This ought to be good!' Shambles said, positioning himself on Ondine's shoulder for a better view of the oncoming fireworks.

Chapter Four

arguerite and the lad sprang apart, their eyes round like golf balls, mouths open in shock. It must have been serious, because Marguerite's normally perfect hair looked tousled. For a long second, it seemed like nothing would happen, but Ondine knew it was only the kind of lull that heralded something ominous, like the stillness in time between a bolt of lightning and the resulting thunder clap.

The young man stood up first, ran his hand through his short brown hair, straightened his rumpled jacket, then extended his trembling palm towards Josef to shake his hand. Josef offered nothing in return.

The lad let his hand drop, along with the expression on his face. 'Mr de Groot, this isn't what it looks like. I have nothing but the most honourable intentions towards your daughter.'

'Good opening gambit,' Shambles said. 'It'll buy him five seconds before yer da runs him through.'

'Who are you?' Josef asked. It sounded like he was talking through gritted teeth.

'Da, please, calm down. That's no way to treat your future son-in-law,' Marguerite pleaded.

'My *what?*'

In the darkness, it was hard to tell, but Da's face was probably close to purple.

'Sir,' the lad started again, holding his hand forward for the second time, which was a pretty gutsy gesture, given the circumstances. 'My name is Thomas Berger and I would like your permission to marry your daughter Marguerite.'

A sharp intake of breath was all Ondine could manage, such was her shock. Marguerite? Engaged? Already?

'Aw, *the nice*!' Shambles said. 'They're in looove.'

Finally, Josef extended his hand to Thomas but it wasn't a shake. More like a death grip. An awkward silence ensued.

Everyone looked to the ground. Margi scrunched her hands in her lap.

'I don't appreciate being kept in the dark,' Da said at last.

'Maybe if you didn't fly off the handle all the time, we wouldn't have to keep secrets,' Margi said.

Go Margi!

'What are you doing out here?' The voice came from the back door, and they turned as one to see Ma standing on the threshold. 'Back inside all of you, there's work to be done. Oh, hello there, Thomas dear, how are you?'

Another sharp intake of breath made Ondine's lungs fit to burst.

'Good thanks, Mrs G,' the young man replied. His familiar tone with Ma told everyone this relationship with Marguerite must have been going on for a while. This latest revelation left Ondine light-headed with equal portions of excitement and confusion.

'Lovely.' Ma turned to the rest of the party. 'Josef? In here please, I need you to tap the next keg. Margi, when you're ready you can relieve Cybelle at the bar.

Oh good, Ondine, you're here too. You can get started on the dishes piling up in the sink.'

'This isn't finished, young lady,' Josef warned Marguerite as she headed for the relative safety of the public bar. Her father wouldn't dare upset the patrons but that didn't stop him from venting his anger in the relative quiet of the hallway. 'This isn't finished by a long shot.'

'Show's over, but nawt for long I bet,' Shambles said as he and Ondine headed for the kitchen, where teetering towers of greasy plates awaited. 'I'm really warming to your da. I've met plenty like him. Such good fun. Thought he'd pop a blood vessel.'

'Hush up, Shambles, or I'll use you as a dishcloth,' Ondine warned.

Later that night – actually, it was early the next morning – after they'd guided the last patrons out, locked the doors, mopped the floors, wiped the bar, washed the dishes, locked the takings in the safe under the kitchen floorboards and turned out the lights, everything descended into quiet.

A tense kind of quiet, judging by the looks that had passed between Marguerite and her ma, and then from Ma to Da.

Cybelle tucked her straight bob behind her ears as she helped Ondine dry and polish the last of the cutlery. 'Wouldn't mind being a fly on the wall tonight, eh, Ondi?'

'Good idea.' Shambles took his leave from Ondine's shoulder and disappeared in a blur of black fur up the back stairs towards their parents' quarters.

'For once, I'm glad I'm not the oldest,' Ondine said. 'Margi's really taking one for the team tonight.'

'Da will get over it. He just has to get used to the fact we're not babies any more,' Cybelle said.

'Lucky we're not Catholic, or he'd have shipped us off to the nunnery.'

'Don't give him ideas. He'd convert us all in a heartbeat,' Cybelle said with a soft giggle.

The chink and clunk of silverware (not sterling silverware, this was the cheaper kind) muffled their conversation. In any case, Ma and Da would be too caught up in 'the Marguerite situation' to pay them much heed, so they could keep talking.

'So, what's going on with you and Shambles?' Cybelle asked.

Ondine dropped her fork. 'Wh-at do you mean?'

'Come on, Ondi. I've seen you listening to him. He talks to you, doesn't he? And you talk back.'

Cybelle's pale brown eyes looked so dramatic under all that eyeliner and thick fringe. They positively bored into Ondine's soul. Despite her earlier brush with deceit at the Duke's house, Ondine found it impossible to lie to her sister.

'So far only Ma and I can hear him. Ma knows who he is – he used to be a real young man once. He was the Laird of Glen Logan, and he knew Great Aunt Col, back when she was our age.'

'You mean Witchy Woman?' Cybelle's eyes gleamed and her eyebrows disappeared under her fringe.

It was their secret name for their great aunt, not that they ever said so within adult hearing.

'Shh, Aunty Col can get very upset when she's offended,' Ondine said, then she relayed an abridged version of how Aunty Col had treated Shambles, after the way Shambles had behaved at the debutante ball, which only made Cybelle's eyes gleam even more.

'So, how old is Shambles? He'd have to be eighty at least if he was around when Old Col was young.'

'That's the lucky bit. Thanks to Old Col's spell, he hasn't a hair of grey on him, and he's so sprightly. He acts more like he's our age,' Ondine said with a shrug of her shoulders as she dried the last spoon. She picked up the cutlery and clunked it all in the drawers. 'Phew, that's it for the night. I'm fair knackered.'

'You're what?' Cybelle asked.

'Just something Shambles says.'

When Ondine and Cybelle tucked themselves into their beds later that night, Shambles leapt into the room and dived for Ondine, snuggling into the warmth of her neck.

'What are you doing, Shambles? You're supposed to sleep in the laundry,' Ondine said as his soft warm fur caressed her skin. It wasn't right to have a man in her bed, but then Shambles wasn't really a *real* man as such, so perhaps that made it OK. What with all the shocks and revelations today, she barely knew what to think. And he wasn't really in the bed, it was more like sharing a pillow, and where was the harm in that?

'Aye, but the laundry's mockit.[17] This is the nice.'

'He's talking to you, isn't he? What's he saying?' Cybelle whispered.

'I have no idea. He's reverted to Scottish.'

'Aw, lass, I like ye, because ye feed me leftovers and cold stovies.[18] As a return favour, I'll tell ye everything your parents said about Marguerite when they thought no one was listening.'

In a few hours' time, after the sun came up, there would be an attempt on the Duke's life at the station. But right now Ondine was more interested in dramas closer to home.

'Yer da says she's too young, but he can't see that ye've all grown up and he can't control ye any more. Yer ma was more circumspect,' Shambles said as he made himself comfortable on Ondine's pillow. 'She says Thomas would move in and then they'd have an

---

17 *Filthy and disgusting. Like armpits and roadkill.*
18 *Leftovers from the stove. Builds up the immune system.*

extra pair of hands at the bar, and Margi wouldnae work out front any more and be leered on by drunks. Sure and it would be better if she married and stayed close to home, than married and ran away.[19] She also said she'd get a refund on the Summercamp, owing to the fact you'll be needed here now and won't be going back.'

Ondine shook her head as a wry smile crept over her lips. 'Trust Ma to appeal to his practical side.' Secretly she felt glad her mother wanted her back.

'What did he say?' Cybelle asked.

The wry smile turned into a huff. 'I feel like a parrot, having to repeat everything. Shambles, how come Ma and I can hear you and Cybelle can't?'

A cheeky look crossed Shambles's face and he winked

---

19 *The average age for a first marriage in Brugel is one of the lowest in Europe. It's 22.4 for men and 21.1 for women, so Marguerite is bang on average. In Poland it is 26.2 for men, 23 for women. Sweden is 32.9 for men, 30.4 for women. Brugel's positively medieval welfare system for single parents also makes it a more secure option for a woman to be in a marriage before having children. There is no single-parent pension. Somebody really should do something about it.*

The link between early age of first marriage and lack of anything decent on television is yet to be proved.

at Ondine. 'Because you're the fairest in the land.'

A giggle percolated in her tummy, but she held it in check. 'Um, he's not sure,' she said, feeling a little embarrassed at the compliment.

High time to switch off the light – that way Cybelle wouldn't be able to see Ondine grinning. Cybelle also wouldn't be able to see how furiously she was blushing, judging by the heat pouring through her neck and face as the man in ferret form cuddled against her skin.

'So, what next?' Cybelle asked.

Shambles relayed what he heard to Ondine, and Ondine relayed what she heard to Cybelle. 'Yer ma wants the wedding to happen as soon as possible. They're planning an engagement party, and yer da will have to get used to having another man around the hoose.'

For a moment Ondine wondered what it would be like having an older brother. Except it wouldn't really be like having an older brother, because Thomas would be much too polite to boss her around like a real older brother would.

'Yer da's main concern is that all of this will give

you and Cybelle ideas,' Shambles added. 'He thinks it will set a bad example, but Thomas isnae gonna stoat the ba'.[20] Your ma had an answer for that too – she said, "How can it be a bad example if they're married?" She said it was only natural that married people should live together. It was either that or Margi and Thomas elope and live somewhere else, and then we'd be short one barmaid slash kitchen hand slash laundry girl. We'd have to bring in more outside help, and that would mean paying proper wages.'

They thought about this for a little while, until Cybelle said, 'Don't you think it's strange? Da couldn't wait for us to grow up so we'd be able to help out more. But now that we are older he's treating us like babies.'

'I know. It's driving me crazy. Was he always like this or am I just noticing it more?' Ondine asked the darkness.

Shambles piped up, 'I'd say it's a bit of both. Dads are the same the world over. When their babies grow

---

20 *'Stoat the ba" is when a man and a woman love each other very much and have a very special cuddle. Only in this case the woman is very young and isn't yet legally supposed to be having those sorts of cuddles. And the man is well aware of that fact.*

up and start getting interested in other people, they realise every other randy lad out there is just like they used to be. I guess it's part of the circle of life.'

Ondine didn't see it like that. 'I think that's what they call hypocrisy. Da just wants it all his own way.'

'Then you should let him think he's getting it,' Shambles muttered.

Despite the late hour, Ondine couldn't stop her mind from racing. Injustice did that to a girl.

'Good on Ma for standing up for Margi,' Cybelle said. 'By the time they get round to me, it will be much easier, and when it's your turn, Ondi, they'll be so worn down they won't protest.'

That caught Ondine by surprise. 'What do you mean? What's going on with you?'

'Oh, um, you know, I was just talking hypothetically. Goodnight.' And with that, the middle daughter rolled over to face the wall and pretended to sleep. Except she wasn't asleep because Ondine didn't hear any snoring.

'She's a dark horse, that one,' Shambles said, having a chuckle. The giggly movement of his body tickled Ondine's neck. Margi had kept a big secret, and she'd kept it very well. Maybe Belle knew how to keep a secret too. And what about Ondine's turn? Who would she fall in love with? she wondered. For some reason, Lord Vincent's handsome face popped into her mind.

The search for answers about her sisters' secrets kept Ondine awake for another few minutes, before she succumbed to a mixture of fatigue and the soporific effect of Shambles's warm, furry body against her and fell asleep.

When the sun came up, there was little time to think about personal matters, as the Duke's impending doom sat heavily with Ondine and Shambles. Josef was at his overprotective fatherly best, refusing Ondine permission to attend the grand opening of the pedestrian overpass at the station.

'I need to know what happens, so I can see whether our warning helped the Duke. I mean, what's the point of us spending all those hours worried about him if we can't see the outcome for ourselves?' Ondine protested as she returned to the kitchen from the dining room. They were in the midst of the breakfast service for the hotel's guests, so they worked and talked at the same time. Something they were very good at.

Da was having none of it. 'One, it's potentially dangerous. Two, you have a job to do. Look at all those dishes by the sink – they'll not clean themselves.'

Nothing could be further from the truth, Ondine thought, as her hands clenched into angry fists at her sides. The bit about ditching work, that is. The rest of it was true. Dishes never cleaned themselves.

More plates of bacon, sausages, eggs and toast were ready, so Ondine took those out to a table. When she came back, her dad still looked cross.

'Let her go, Da,' Cybelle interjected. 'You could go with Ondi if you're that worried about her safety. I'll stay and help Chef with food prep for the lunch crowds.'

Chef, who had a real name but nobody used it, was the only true employee at the hotel. As such he was the only one who could be fired. He was tall yet light on his feet as he moved about the kitchen cooking meals and stirring sauces. He wore the same bleached-white uniform every day, although he would need a new one soon judging by the way his pot belly strained against the buttons. Under his white hat flecks of jet-black hair poked out, contrasting sharply with his pale skin.[21] All the while the family argued (although they'd deny it was an argument, they'd say it was just debating things, long and heartily, and a bit loudly), Chef stayed out of the line of fire. With his strong and fast hands, he kept busy with another batch of scrambled eggs.

A soft chuckle sounded on Ondine's shoulder. It came from Shambles. *He must be enjoying himself,* she thought, a little puzzled. Maybe Shambles liked a bit of argy-bargy?

Ondine cajoled her father again. At times she felt like exploding with frustration. 'Please let me go, Da.'

'We both know someone out there . . .' her father pointed in the direction of the train station, as if they

---

21 *Chefs work long and odd hours. They are awake at night and catch up on sleep during the day. It's rare for them to get out much, or to see the sun. Just as you should never trust a thin chef (because if they're not eating their food, neither should you), you should never trust a chef with a tan.*

didn't know where it was '. . . wants to kill the Duke.
It's dangerous. What kind of father would I be if I
exposed my daughter to that kind of peril? The safest
thing for us to do is to stay here.'

Was he being deliberately daft? If Ondine's eyes
could roll any further into her head, she'd be looking
into her brain. As much as she tried to keep a cool
head, her pulse skipped up a notch and her clenched
fists wanted to pummel something. 'You've got it all
wrong, Da. Nobody's going to be interested in us.
We'll stay out of the way. I want to see the people who
planned this get caught. I want to see them hauled
away, and when that happens, it might be nice if the
Duke perhaps caught sight of us and acknowledged
our help.'

'You mean if Lord Vincent caught sight of you,'
Josef countered.

'You're impossible!' Ondine clenched and
unclenched her fists in impotent fury. Up until this
point, she hadn't even thought of Vincent. Well, not
much anyway, and what chance he'd even be there?
Pretty slim, she suspected.

'It's a fiddler's biddin'[22] then,' Shambles said behind her ear, which didn't help at all.

'I thought you'd have a bit more natural curiosity about you.' Ondine tried one more time to bend her father's will to her own. 'We spent all that time last night warning him, and now you're not even interested to see how it turns out? What if by being there, we can stop it somehow? There could even be a reward in it for you.'

'Aye, and then yer arse'll fall awf!'[23] Shambles said, rumbling with laughter.

A terse silence filled the kitchen, broken only by the sound of Chef cracking eggs into the poaching pan.

Her father practically glowered at her. 'You're that keen, aren't you? Fine, we'll go, but we're not staying more than half an hour. Then it's straight back to work for you.'

Tension fell away from Ondine's shoulders, making her feel taller and lighter. 'Thank you, Da.' She kissed

---

22 *'A fiddler's biddin'' is a last-minute invitation.*
23 *To say this is flat-out rude. It means 'you're talking pish'. Keep track of these; there'll be a test later on.*

him firmly on the cheek, then gave him a huge hug, nearly knocking Shambles off her shoulder in the process. A broad smile split her face. 'This is going to be so exciting!'

Chapter Five

A huge crowd gathered that morning at the railway station, bringing a carnival atmosphere to something that was normally, well, pedestrian. The smell of fried onions and sausages at the fund-raising stalls filled the air, making Ondine's stomach rumble. Buskers entertained the crowds and played violins and accordions. Women dressed as fairies did a roaring trade painting children's faces in lurid colours.

'I'm off to get me some sausage.' Shambles leapt off Ondine's shoulder and disappeared into the milling crowd in a blur of black.

'No, Shambles, wait!'

Too late, the ferret was gone. *Damn that impetuous bampot*, she thought, borrowing one of his words to suit her means.

'Right then, let's get a good position so we can see the Duke cut the ribbon,' Da said, holding Ondine by the hand. This only served to take her further from where she last saw Shambles.

'Hang on, Da, Shambles has run off. I need to find him,' she said, trying to tamp down the rising sense of panic in her gut.

'He'll be fine. Come on.' Squeezing through the crowd, Da found them a good vantage spot, where they could see the Duke standing at the podium, a pair of scissors in his hands. Standing beside him was a woman of indeterminate age. She had that caught-in-a-wind-tunnel look about her, with arched eyebrows that looked like they were trying to run away from her. Sunlight sparkled off the tiara that sat on her blonde head. Under her arm, she held a furry white dog.

'Is that the Duchess?' Ondine asked.

Da laughed out loud. 'She wishes! No love, that's the Infanta, the Duke's oldest sister.'

'She looks so fancy!' Ondine saw more sparkles of sunlight – even the little dog had jewels in its collar. The thought of the small animal having such a fancy collar made her wonder about Shambles, and whether he might look quite handsome with sparkles around his neck.

Another chuckle from her father. 'Fancy is one way to put it. A bit overdone perhaps. She might have been Duchess if her little brother wasn't born.'

The crowd milled about them and someone stepped on Ondine's foot. A ripple of worry rippled through her. Shambles could easily be trampled in the crush.

'Da, we need to find Shambles.'

'He'll be wherever the food is. Now hush, let's listen to what the Duke —'

Shots rang out. Real gunshots that were so loud you'd swear someone had smacked you on the inside of your head with a brick.

People screamed.

'Get down!' Da yelled. With a jolt he pulled Ondine to the ground, shielding her body with his.

Confusion and turmoil took hold. Everyone around them crouched down, huddling in fear. Noise and screaming filled the sky. Police officers blew their whistles. From a gap under her father's arm, Ondine saw a man running away down the street.

People say that when a big, scary event happens, it takes place in slow motion. In this case, nothing could be further from the truth as it all took place at lightning speed. The police closed in, chased down the culprit for half a block, then tackled him into submission.

'They got him!' Ondine said with relief.

The Duke must have taken their warning seriously. He must have organised more police. Ready to pounce at the slightest provocation.

For the next few minutes everyone stayed low to the ground as the police rounded up another two suspects. With her heartbeat hammering in her ears, Ondine heard her father say something. She couldn't make out the exact words because her ears were still ringing from the gunshots.

'I said, "They've given the all-clear,"' Josef said even louder this time.

But still nobody moved. Well, why would they? Only moments ago shots had rung out above their heads. From their crouched position, Ondine looked around to where the Duke was, to see if the show would go on. The Infanta remained huddled behind a chair. The Duke was on his feet, looking perplexed. In his hand was his traditional three-cornered hat, only now it had a bullet-sized hole through the top of it.

'Ohmygosh! They nearly killed him,' Ondine said, her heart still beating far too quickly.

Josef wrapped his arms around her and held her close, kissing the top of her head. 'Now do you see why I didn't want you to come here? If anything happened to you, I'd never forgive myself.'

'Thanks, Da.' She wanted to say, 'You worry too much,' but in the present circumstances, his worries were perfectly justified.

'I love you so much, my darling girl. And I know you're all grown up now, but I can't help it. To me, you'll always be my baby and that's just how it is.'

'It's OK.' Ondine returned the hug, not caring that he'd called her a baby. At this moment, she'd forgive him just about anything. Trembles rippled through her body as she let the shock take hold. 'I love you too, Da.'

So much remained unsaid as they embraced. Ondine nearly suffocated in the crushing hug but she didn't care. As a father, he suffocated her in so many ways but right now she wasn't complaining.

To their surprise, the Duke indicated he'd carry on with the ceremony. The mere fact that he was bodily unharmed brought many more people to their feet. The cheers ringing in Ondine's ears told her they'd done the right thing. They'd warned the Duke, he'd organised police protection and the crowd had witnessed a nasty scare rather than an assassination.

'Right then,' the Duke called out, gathering his composure and dusting himself off. He picked up the enormous ceremonial scissors and held the blades apart. 'I declare this new pedestrian access open.'

What an amazing man. Ondine marvelled at how quickly he'd recovered his senses. By now she and Josef were on their feet too. The Infanta, however, kept her distance from the podium.

With a gracious nod, the Duke cut the ribbon and the two halves of fabric fluttered to the ground. People applauded, probably with gladness but also a great deal of relief. A group of schoolchildren cheered and raced on to the overpass. They reached the highest point and threw coloured streamers into the crowd.

The Duke acknowledged the gathering. 'Thank you, everyone, for coming. Now, if you'll excuse me, I need a drink!'

The crowd laughed and cheered again, and Ondine could only marvel once more at how well he'd recovered. His poise in the face of such danger seriously impressed her, and she couldn't stop smiling. If she'd been the one in the firing line, she would have been a gibbering mess like the Infanta. But that Duke, wow, what composure!

There was little time to think further about this, because at that moment Da spotted Lord Vincent standing near his father's entourage.

Josef grabbed his daughter's hand. 'Time we got back.' Without further explanation, he led her down the road towards their hotel.

Ondine stole a glance over her shoulder for Shambles and thought, *I hope he's all right.*

In the next glance she saw the Duke and (oh goody!)

Lord Vincent, following them to the pub. Something jumped in her chest, as if her heart suddenly had to beat double time to keep up with rapidly unfolding events.

'Hey, Da, when the Duke said he needed a drink, he was serious. They're right behind us.'

'In that case, we'd better get straight back to the bar so they can have that drink.'

'But where is Shambles? He won't know where we are if we run off and leave him,' Ondine said, trying to hide the panic in her voice. How would one little ferret cope in such chaos? All on his own?

'I wouldn't worry about Shambles, he knows he's on to a good thing with you. He'll find his way home.'

'But, Da, he could get trampled to death. Or worse. Someone could steal him!' A fluttering sense of panic took hold of Ondine. Wrenching her arm free, she turned away from Josef and scanned the streets for any sign of black fur.

'For goodness' sake! He's just a ferret. If he doesn't come home, I'll get you another one. Now hurry up before we're overrun by the mob.' His firm hand gripped Ondine's upper arm, dragging her at a fast clip towards the pub's front door. They hardly ever entered by the main door. In this case her father made an exception, lest the patrons get into the pub before they did.

'But he's not just a ferret, Da, he's a real man! He's only in ferret form because Great-Aunt Col turned him into one!' Ondine yelped as they stumbled across the threshold. 'He needs me or he won't survive!'

'He's a *what?*' Josef's eyes grew round like golf balls. If golf balls were lined with red squiggles from stress.

There was no moisture in her throat when she swallowed. Oh dear. Now she'd blown it. And she had his full attention so there was no getting out of it. A pulse trembled at her neck as Josef stared her down. The secret was out and she had nobody to blame but herself. Her sisters knew how to keep secrets; why couldn't she?

'Oh good, you're back,' Ma said from the doorway, breaking the tableau.

A sigh of relief escaped Ondine's lips and she felt her shoulders sag. God bless Ma's incredible sense of timing!

'No, dear, you're not interrupting me this time,' Da said sternly.

Caught in the spotlight of her father's stare, Ondine felt her tongue turn to sandpaper. A squeak came out instead of words.

'Well, she'd better be quick,' Ma said, looking out through the large front windows. 'Is that the Duke of Brugel heading this way, with about two hundred followers?' She turned and headed towards the kitchen. 'Chef! Cybelle! Margi! Thomas! All hands on deck – the whole city's coming for lunch.'

'I thought that ferret was a ferret, pure and simple,' the head of the de Groot household said. Only moments earlier he'd been cuddling Ondine and telling her how much he loved her. Now he looked like he could happily have her sectioned.

'I'm sorry, Da. Shambles was a man once, and Old Col turned him into a ferret because he got drunk at her debutante ball.'

'And what? You just forgot to tell me?'

A confusing sickness took hold of Ondine, spreading out from her heart and filling her body, right down to her boots. Before she could respond, they heard multiple footsteps on the path outside.

Time was against them and Da had to let the situation drop so he could make ready with the beer. Any relief Ondine could have felt from her reprieve was quickly replaced by concern for Shambles. Then her concern for Shambles was quickly replaced by excitement at the appearance of the Duke of Brugel and his son Lord Vincent in the hotel's doorway.

Something light and fizzy stirred inside Ondine. Just from looking at Vincent. Because he was so very lovely to look at.

No time to gaze, they had work to do. To help with the crowd, Margi, Thomas and Josef all tended bar, and Ondine felt seriously impressed at how well they worked together. Like they'd been doing it for years. She had to hand it to Margi, the older girl had held her ground – as had Thomas from the look of things. But as much as Ondine thought she should be worrying about her sister and her prospective brother-in-law, she couldn't keep her mind from straying to thoughts of Shambles, and where he could be.

You may have heard the expression 'chick magnet', which is a term applied to a handsome man who draws women – or chicks – to him. Just as a regular magnet attracts paperclips and iron filings, seemingly without any effort. In fact, this is one of the elemental forces of nature at work, and is one of the easier aspects of physics to understand. Shambles the ferret was no chick magnet, but he was a trouble magnet, with an uncanny knack for attracting and finding trouble. You could say his knack for attracting trouble was also an elemental force of nature.

The moment he slipped away from Ondine's shoulder that morning, he followed his nose to the smell of frying sausages from one of the fund-raising stalls along the railway platform. The onions he didn't care for, but the sausages made his mouth water.[24] A plan formulated in his head – stay close to people near the barbecue and hot plates and sausages will drop from the sky.

Soon, a suitable leg presented itself, with sturdy shoes and thick denim pants, making it easy for Shambles to get a grip. Before its owner could finish yelping, 'What's on my leg?' he'd dropped his sausage, bread, onions and mustard on the ground. Shambles jumped free and launched himself towards his prize, grabbed it in his teeth and disappeared behind the stall. And oh, it was bliss, eating a sausage that was half as long as his body. The hot fat dripped over his chin. Chunks of meat-ish mince slid down his throat and warmed his belly. In another few chomps, all that remained of the meal was a smear of grease on his black fur.

A clever person, perhaps even a not-so-clever person, might feel satisfied with that score and leave well

---

24 *Ferrets require a diet high in protein and fat, and low in carbohydrates. Sausages fit the bill nicely, provided they are not filled with breadcrumbs. Sausages can also become a bit tedious. It doesn't matter what you do with a sausage or how many herbs or semi-sundried tomatoes you add, after a while they all taste the same.*

enough alone. Not Shambles. Filled with confidence at how well his first attempt had gone, he reasoned a second attempt would be even more successful.

He didn't have to wait long for another mark. This man had pants made from a thick canvas type material (Shambles hadn't studied fashion, so didn't know silk from sawdust) and a satchel on his side that made an excellent hitching post for a ferret to dig his claws and fangs into. In a heartbeat Shambles raced up his leg, grabbed on to the bag and opened his mouth to catch the sausage.

Then it all went horribly wrong.

The satchel opened and a gun fell out. Helpless, Shambles watched the weapon drop to the ground. It discharged on impact. His world split apart with the loudest sound he'd ever heard. Everyone screamed. Shambles hit a nearby wall with a thud and kept falling, his arms scrabbling for something to hang on to on the way down. His claws caught in a thick material – the man's pants – and he clung on hard, lurching back and forth with momentum as the man ran off. Nasty hot bile filled the back of his throat. His ears filled with screams. Then a whistle blew and heavy footsteps closed in. Several pairs of footsteps.

From the corner of his eye, Shambles saw a policeman lunge towards them. He let go of the leg, fell hard on the pavement, and his world turned black.

Back at the pub, things were so busy in the dining room the piano stood silent. Cybelle worked in the kitchen beside Chef, while Ondine and Colette took orders and served food.

'Ondi, take these meals to table twelve,' Cybelle said, before she rushed back to the stove to remove a tray of savoury tarts.

Her arms loaded with food (two plates balanced on one arm, a third plate on the other), Ondine took her orders and walked to the designated table. That's when she saw Lord Vincent sitting at the head of it. Not that she was going to drop the plates or anything, but the sight of him nearly made her miss a step. He looked ruffled and gorgeous; his sun-kissed, dark blond hair was all messed up but his brown eyes were clear and bright, and trained on her.

Heat crept up Ondine's neck at the thought of him checking her out.

'It's Ondine, isn't it? That's a beautiful name,' Vincent said, extending his hand in friendship.

Something turned to liquid inside her.

Being polite, Ondine served Vincent and his companions their meals, then took his hand to give it a friendly shake. Her skin tingled at his warm touch. How long should they hold hands for? Would it be rude to pull away? Then he did something that made her insides go completely gooey. Eyes still locked with hers, Vincent turned her hand over and kissed the inside of her wrist.

The touch of his tender lips against her skin was the most erotic thing Ondine had ever experienced.

Heat shot up her arm, darted into her heart and pinged all around her body. Until this moment, she'd loved the feeling of just looking at him. Now he'd kissed her and she felt something strange, wonderful and new lurch low in her belly.

Ondine wasn't really sure what it was, but she knew she liked it.

Chapter Six

A whole week later and there was no sign of Shambles. Not a skerrick.[25] For a teenage girl with an overactive imagination, it was a complete disaster. Visions of Shambles lying dead in a city gutter filled Ondine's mind. That's if he was already dead. He might have been carried off by a hawk, his limbs ripped off while he yet lived, to be shoved down the hungry mouths of chicks. Or some revolting child might have found him and taken him home, where she'd be half strangling him to death with affection, then putting a bonnet on his head so that he matched the rest of her dollies! Ondine found herself thinking of Shambles

---

25 *The spell checker thinks this should be 'cleric' but religion has nothing to do with this. 'Skerrick' means scrap, as in scrap of paper, scrap of cloth or scrap of information.*

far too much. Thinking how vulnerable and small he was. Other times she found herself wondering what he might look like as a proper man. If she could find a way to turn him human again, would she like the end result? Would he be as handsome as Lord Vincent?

All the anxiety meant her appetite paid the price – she could barely eat for worry at breakfast. Then she became ravenous around lunchtime and found herself eating scraps off people's returned plates.[26]

It had also been a week of astonishing busyness and flat-out-edness. Business had never been so good, all because the Duke and his dishy son had come to their pub after the ballyhoo at the station.

I'll never wash my wrist again. Ondine cast her mind back to that lush kiss on her tender skin. How she'd blushed furiously in front of Vincent and his gang, and the way he'd looked at her with an unreadable but unquestionably exciting-and-a-little-bit-dangerous

---

26 *Always have a big breakfast. It gets the metabolism going for the day and helps you think straight. Skip breakfast and you lose ten IQ points.*

expression. That promise vanished after she had to roll up her sleeves and get stuck into the washing-up.

Laundry duty washed away another layer of skin, so really, all she had were memories. But oh, what lovely memories. His soft, warm lips brushing her skin, his walnut-brown eyes fixed on hers, her heart racing nineteen to the dozen. Even now, as she thought of him, her pulse increased. While folding sheets and tablecloths and pillowcases, Ondine kept seeing the lovely Lord Vincent's smiling eyes. Finishing with the folding, she made sure no one was looking and dared to kiss herself in the same spot.

What a let-down! No sensations at all, just the feeling that she must look like an idiot. Thank goodness nobody had seen her. Not even Shambles, to make her feel like a twit for entertaining such thoughts.

And Lord Vincent hadn't been back to their dining room all week, which was such a shame. Ondine felt sure that he'd be back in a day or two. Three at the most.

A sudden cry of anguish echoed through the kitchen, which sounded suspiciously like Ma having a conniption.

'I don't believe it! They can't write such things! How dare they publish this! Josef, get a lawyer, let's sue them! This is all lies. Lies, lies, lies! Call themselves a newspaper? This is a rag. It's not fit for the toilet!'

'Ma, what's wrong?' Ondine called out, as she hot-footed her way towards the centre of the family storm. When she got to the kitchen, she found everyone standing around the island bench, reading an article from the *Weekend Hacienda Leisure Guide*.

Somebody had written a review of their hotel. And it wasn't very nice. The food and wine critic, known by the pseudonym *Dee Gustation*, had gone to town on them.

'But when was she here?' Cybelle asked. 'I never saw anyone with a notebook in the dining room. Did you, Ondi?'

'Nope, and everyone's been really nice as well. Nobody's even sent any food back, which is a good thing, right?' Ondine asked.

'We haven't seen anyone in the bar who might be a critic, have we, Thomas?' Marguerite added. Thomas shook his head.

Thomas was crowding around the table along with the rest of the family, his pale hair contrasting sharply with the family of brunettes. Where had he come from? Everyone kept talking, so Ondine bent her head at a funny angle (the page was upside down, so it took all her concentration) to read the article.

Dangerous Dining Adventures

A night at The Station Hotel is a true adventure in dining, where the faint-hearted need not apply.

Let's begin with our first brush with death – the table wine. Called such because its only true use should be for cleaning the tables at the end of the night.

This is a hotel with a family atmosphere, which extends to the guests – in such a way that those in the dining room can easily become caught up in domestic disputes emanating from the kitchen.

Despite this, the food – when it does eventually arrive – is edible. That is what little you can find under the sea of gravy.

The beer is suitably cold, chilled from the frosty stares of the publican/overprotective father who has no issue with using his beautiful daughters for slave labour. In many museums, you can look but not touch – here, don't even look at the daughters lest the father turns you into a block of ice with just one glance.

Towards the end of the evening, the rousing music from a talented but frustrated concert pianist is a fitting way to end the night. The raucous clamour from the piano and singing elder sister distracts everyone from the noises made by patrons in gastric distress outside in the gutter.

'Oh, I can't bear it!' Ma said as she wiped tears from her cheeks with the back of her hand. 'Who could be so cruel to us?'

'Someone who is jealous of our success,' Da said.

From where Ondine stood, she figured her father's guess was as good as anyone else's.

A sad kind of quiet descended in the kitchen, which was pretty remarkable considering there were seven people all hunched around the table, reading the newspaper.

'I'll go to the paper's office and find out who wrote

this,' Marguerite said. 'I'll explain that they're wrong. I'll invite the reviewer back so she can write something positive about us.'

'Or make up something worse!' Josef said.

'Hey, look, Da,' Ondine said, trying to change the subject. 'Here's a story about the people who tried to shoot the Duke. They've written a fair bit . . . they've charged three men and . . . what does "diplomatic immunity" mean?'

'It means they've got a good lawyer,' Josef said with a sniff of disgust.

The telephone rang, making them all jump. For a moment nobody wanted to answer it, then Ma straightened her posture, brushed her hair back, and made to pick it up.

'Station Hotel, good morning . . . Yes . . . I see . . . Yes, of course . . . No, no problem at all, thank you for calling and letting us know. Have a lovely day.'

Ma put the receiver down on to the cradle and shuddered. 'That was the van Nyuus booking,[27] cancelling for tonight. Cybelle, you're better on the

---

27 *It was for twelve people.*

phone than me, can you take the rest of the calls? I'm going to lie down for a mo—'

A streak of black fur barrelled into the kitchen, ran under the table and up Ondine's leg.

'Shambles! Oh, Shambles, my darling, you're alive!' Ondine cried, scooping the bundle of bedraggled fluff into her arms and kissing the top of his messy head. Sparks of joy danced around her heart. He was back!

'As much as I appreciate a kiss from a fair maiden, there's no time for that,' Shambles said as he panted for breath. 'Everyone get to work, the halth inspecta is coming!'

Ma turned white and her chin wobbled in distress. 'Can this day get any worse? Who cares if the health inspector comes? We're done for anyway!'

Josef, Chef, Thomas and Marguerite all turned to Ma, asking variants on the 'what did you say?' theme. Because, of course, they hadn't heard Shambles say anything.

Only Cybelle remained looking at Ondine. The middle daughter instinctively knew, from her mother's screeching reaction, that Shambles had come back with bad news.

Ignoring them all, Ondine cuddled her returned friend. 'Shambles, you stink. Where have you been? You must be starving. Here, have some sausages. Chef, can you grab some bones out of the stockpot?'

Shambles found his voice. 'It's that ungrateful Duke's family. This is all their doing. They're hell-bent on running us out of town! And I'll say yes to the meat too, I'm fair starven.'

Confusion reigned at the table while Shambles virtually inhaled his snack. Ondine patted his back, feeling the corrugated ribs through matted fur.

All eyes turned to Ma, waiting for an answer.

She gave it to them, revealing Shambles's true identity and communication skills.

Da shook his head. 'Now you're saying he can talk? Then why can't I hear him?'

Confusion aplenty. Thanks to the newspaper review, they were already in a state of shock. It was only natural that the news that their ferret could talk and was in fact a real man would completely bowl them all over.

* * *

You'll understand a certain need for brevity at this stage, what with everything being so exciting – plus, you already know the whole story up to now, so you don't need to hear it again. Let's pick this up after the half hour of 'whats?' and 'hows?' to the point where people started to make sense again.

Chef shook his head and said, 'Now I've heard everything.'

Marguerite and Thomas gave each other surprised looks.

Da's jaw clamped shut and Ondine could tell, just from his expression, that his mind was already moving on to more important matters: white-hot indignation.

'But we saved that miserable Duke's life!' he spat.

Cybelle chimed in, 'What could he have against us? He came over here after the incident, bringing half of Venzelemma with him. He was having a great time, wasn't he, Ondi?'

Heat seared Ondine's cheeks as she thought about what a great time she'd had, with Lord Vincent kissing her wrist. Her skin still tingled just thinking about it.

'Right then, no time to waste. Let's close the place ourselves and then there's no reason to let the health inspector in,' Ma said, rising from the table and fetching the clutch of keys.

'But we've got guests, and a full house tonight!' Da said, then corrected himself. 'I mean, a nearly full house.'

'We cancel everything, just for a week, and we'll work like stink and get it all sparkling from floor to ceiling. Cancelling the bookings buys us some time and when we re-open, the inspector will be so dazzled by everything he won't be able to find anything to fault. Margi, you and Thomas make up some signs for the front windows to say we're closed for renovations. Belle, you and Chef put on a slap-up lunch for everyone who's still here, as a way of saying thanks and goodbye, for the moment. Ondi, give Shambles a bath, he stinks, then both of you join your da in the bar. We'll start at the front and work our way through the entire place.'

'Colette, my love,' Da said, finally breaking his wife's string of orders, 'how are we to pay for this?'

'We'll find a way. Something will turn up.'

As Shambles finished his third sausage, Ondine offered him some water, which he happily accepted. 'I'm going to give you that bath, Shambles,' she said, and kissed the top of his head again. The acrid stench of dead things flew up her nose. 'Pee-yew, you reek!'

A rumbly laugh escaped Shambles. 'Care to rub me back, lass?'

From across the table, Ma gave the ferret a stern look. 'Shambles, that's not appropriate!'

Shocked, Ondine looked at her mother, face aghast. Jupiter's moons, Ma had good hearing! Then she saw her father's icy cold glare – created not from hearing Shambles, but from guessing what he must have said. A smile formed at the corner of Ondine's mouth. The newspaper article was right in one respect: her dad could chill a whole room with a single glance.

As much as she should feel angry because of her father's mood swings, she felt happy. Shambles was alive and in one (smelly) piece, and for that she was grateful. In a few hours, her father would be over the shock of the news and would return to normal. The best thing for Ondine to do was stay out of his way.

'Thank ye for the food, and for yer concern. It's nice to be missed. I missed ye too,' Shambles whispered as they left the kitchen. 'And by the way, I noticed Cybelle and Chef were touching knees under the table.'

The fresh information sent a bolt of shock through Ondine. 'Belle and Chef? What?'

'That sister of yers is a dark horse,' Shambles chuckled.

Ondine's mind went blank. Not that Belle couldn't have a love interest, but that it would be with Chef. 'I can't get my head around it. But – but he's nearly twice her age. *Belle and Chef?*'

'Sure, and I'm older than ye, but yer about to get me fair nekked in a bath, eh lass?'

Heat scorched Ondine's neck and face again. Thank goodness nobody else was in earshot of the ferret. As much as she'd like to make verbal repartee with him, there was little time for mucking about. Ondine knew they'd be needed for renovations, whatever that entailed, so it was straight up to the bathroom for both of them. Upon reaching the basin, Shambles came over all shy.

'Ah, I'll take it from here if ye don't mind.'

'Don't be silly, you won't even be able to turn on the taps,' Ondine said.

Shambles looked at his options. 'Right then. Well. Close yer eyes.'

'We don't have time for this. You need a bath and I'm giving you one.' Ondine placed the plug in the plughole and set about filling the basin with warm water.

'Right . . . but it's just that . . . I've never had a bath with anyone else before. It's well confronting if ye think about it.'

Ondine laughed. 'But Shambles, come on, you're only . . .'

'Only what? A ferret? Thanks a lot.'

'I didn't mean that.'

Shambles shook his head, 'Thank you. I think. Now, I have to warn you,' he dipped his front paw in the water, 'oh no, that's too hot, more cold water please.'

Ondine did so.

'That's better. Now, I have to warn you about that

Duke and his family. Especially Vincent. He's got it in fer us.'

Ondine dropped the soap, 'Lord Vincent? But he was here with his friends and they had a great time.' She blushed furiously at the memory. The wrist he'd kissed now propped up the black ferret in the basin. He leant against it for support, and she could feel his small heart hammering away.

'He was here? Then it's worse than I thought. Stay away from them, Ondi, they're bad news. They're the ones setting the halth inspecta on to us. They want to close us down. I don't know why yet, but they've got it in fer us.'

Ondine retrieved the soap and scrubbed Shambles's furry back. Time to change the subject.

'Shambles, before you became a ferret, how did you like to do your hair?' He'd look so cute with a big curl on his forehead.

'Eh? I dunno, lass, I jest brushed it. Why d'ye ask?'

'Just wondering,' she said, wondering how he might have done his hair, wondering what colour it had been, wondering whether he was as handsome as Lord

Vincent. 'I mean, was it really long so you had to tie it back or did you cut it short?'

'Short like Lord Vincent's?'

'Yeah,' she said before thinking.

'Aha! So you're thinking of him while you're bathing me, eh lass?'

Mercury's wings! 'No, it's not like that.'

'Really now?'

'Shambles, please. I was actually wondering what *you* looked like.'

'And why might that be? So ye can compare me to Vincent?'

Yes. 'No, not like that. Just that it would be nice if I knew who I was talking to.'

'All right. I used to be fit, like. I had short hair, and all the bits of my face were where they're s'posed to be.'

The description helped. A bit. 'You're lucky I didn't know who you really were, otherwise I might have left you at Psychic Summercamp.'

A stray thought came unbidden – thank goodness she'd come home early from Summercamp, otherwise who knows what might have happened.[28]

After she finished washing and drying him, and he looked and smelled like a proper clean ferret should, she made for the dining room and got to work. She carried chairs and tables out to the rear garden – as soon as guests vacated them – so she could scrub them down in daylight. It was impressive how quickly guests chose to leave the premises once you removed their capacity to sit down.

Shambles ducked under a chair.

'What are you doing?' Ondine asked.

'Gnawing awf thae gobs of chewing gum,' he

---

28 *In a parallel universe, Ondine remained at Psychic Summercamp and failed all her subjects, then returned home to find a pile of smouldering ash where the hotel and her home used to be. Josef had walked into the kitchen and discovered Cybelle and Chef in a passionate embrace. He'd lost his temper and thrown the nearest thing to hand – a jug of water – at the pair of them. The jug missed its target and landed in the roiling deep fryer, which exploded and set the kitchen on fire. They didn't know the health inspector was due to arrive the next morning, but in any case, his visit was a moot point.*

In yet another parallel universe, the health inspector decided to arrive two weeks early and was hit by the 7.05 express as he attempted to cross the train tracks. This was because the pedestrian walkway hadn't opened yet.

replied, sounding like he had a mouth full of the goo already. 'Folks have such filthy habits.'

In the harsh light of day, the timber furniture looked hideous. Many pieces were scratched and dented and some refused to stop wobbling. They looked shoddy.

'Let's do some sorting,' Shambles said. 'The worst of them go by the back shed. We'll take the wee stoppers off the feet and use them on the good stuff.'

'Good idea, Shambles.'

'Aw, thanks, lass. It's nice to feel useful.'

Ondine beamed at the compliment. 'So, you haven't filled me in on where you've been. Care to elaborate?'

'I was fair traumatised by the whole thing. I woke up in the Duke's place. Big and echocy and full of people wearing stompy boots. If I ever go back there, it will be too soon. I found a place to hide and waited for the Duke to return. He did, with Vincent, and all the time I was there, Vincent was saying how they needed to close this place down.'

'But . . . that doesn't make sense. If they hated it, why didn't they say something when they were here?'

'I don't know what their motives are either, lass, but

I know what I heard, and it was Vincent leading the charge. Hey, how come every time I say his name ye get that funny look on yer face?'

'I don't get a funny look.'

'Yes ye do. Lord Vincent.'

Ondine kept her expression as stern as possible.

'I know ye don't want to listen to me, but it's the truth. Lord Vincent is *nawt* to be trusted.'

'I've heard enough,' Ondine said. 'We have work to do.'

She spent the rest of the day scrubbing down timber, polishing the good items and fixing what she could, with Shambles directing her. Ma came out to inspect their work, a beaming smile spreading across her satisfied face.

'I thought I'd have to buy a whole new set, but you've done a marvellous job, you two. Right, when you're finished, come and help us carry out the carpet.'

Just as her mother had ordered, the family were scrubbing their way through the entire building. It meant tearing up the ancient, smelly carpet and exposing the floorboards. Considering the flooring was old, stained and reeked of beer, the renovations were long overdue. By the end of the day they'd done a lot of work, but the place didn't look exactly clean. If anything, they'd stirred up such huge amounts of fetid dust they'd created yet more mess. It was only one day; they were sure to make more mess tomorrow.

Rolling up the carpet had exposed a thick layer of old newspapers. Not the underlay most people had in their homes to create a soft cushion to walk on, contributing to a lovely, homey atmosphere. Like the carpets before them, the newspapers stank of beer and other weird things, so they had to go as well.

'Load them all into the fireplace. We'll have a ritual burning and cleansing ceremony tonight. I hope Auntie Col gets here in time – she'll have some good spells,' Ma said.

'Is Auntie Col coming here tonight?' Shambles asked out loud. 'Could she turn me back?'

Ondine froze for a moment. Shambles wanted to be a real man again. Which meant she'd finally get to see what he looked like. In her mind, she'd begun giving him features she found pleasing. But what if the end result fell short? What if he was – gulp – gobsmackingly ugly? In her heart, she knew that was a selfish way of looking at things. Shambles was entitled to his former life. He should be allowed to be himself again no matter what he looked like.

It's the personality, not the package that counts.

Another sad thought popped into her head. *If Shambles becomes human again, there'll definitely be no more snuggling in bed.*

She shook the imaginings from her mind in the same way she shook the dust from the old curtains.

'Becoming human again is a good idea, Shambles. We could do with the extra manpower,' Ma said.

Typical Ma.

'Hey, look at this,' Marguerite interrupted. She held up a sheet of old newspaper. Because it had been protected from sunlight, the paper had retained its original off-white colour, and the contrasting black text was easy to read. 'It's an obituary of the old Duke of Brugel. Must be the current Duke's father. Oh, and it's a juicy one too. Listen to this: it says he died without having to answer to charges of embezzlement.'

'Keep hold of that. It might come in handy,' Da said.

'So might this,' Thomas said, lifting up a section of exposed floorboard. 'There's something down here.'

Working together, Da and Thomas pulled up another two boards. All of them were cut into short lengths, as if designed to come away together.

In the cobwebby recesses beneath the bar-room floor lay a large metal box. It reminded Ondine of the deposit box in the kitchen, where they put all their money for safe-keeping until the banks opened on Monday.[29] The mysterious box was so heavy they called in Chef to help them lift it out. The men grunted and groaned, pulled it free with an 'oomph', then dropped the box at their feet.

---

29 In Brugel banks are open on Mondays from 10 a.m. to 3 p.m., Tuesdays from 4 p.m. to 7 p.m., Thursdays and Fridays from 11 a.m. to 6 p.m. Closed Wednesdays and weekends.

As an interesting side note to history, Brugel's Prime Minister vetoed Euros after he saw the first pressing of Brugel's 20-cent Euro coin featuring a banker in a hammock. The coins were withdrawn from circulation, but are available for bids over US$20 on eBay. Bidders should contact user profile pmforlifeme for more details.

More dust billowed.

A tingle of excitement crept into Ondine's throat – and it wasn't just the dust – as she began to imagine what might be in the box.

'What's in it?' Marguerite asked the hushed room.

In a flash, Shambles dropped down from Ondine's shoulder and clambered on to the box, chewing at its leather straps until they came free. Thomas and Josef lifted the lid. Their mouths fell open. So did Ondine's. And Ma's, and Marguerite's. Even Shambles's wee furry mouth, full of nippy fangs and a little pink tongue, gaped in shock.

'Saturn's rings!' Ondine gasped.

'Looks like we've found a way to pay for the renovations,' Da said.

'What did I tell you? I knew Shambles would bring us good luck,' Ma said.

Chapter Seven

The contents of the box gleamed in the afternoon sunlight shining through the front windows. Gold rings. Bracelets. Fine threads of necklaces studded with diamonds. Brooches. Earrings with drop pearls. A tiara with red gems that might have been rubies – Ondine couldn't tell. Not a tangled mess, as you might expect, but all sorted and segmented into neat little compartments. Underneath the tray of gleaming jewellery they found wads of banknotes, stamped with faces and places on them, which Ondine didn't recognise. They must have been made before the currency changed.[30]

---

30 *Prior to decimal currency, Brugel had a brief period of cinquimal currency. Five Drops to the Schlip, five Schlips to the Pennig, five Pennigs to the Lipp. The closest equivalent of the Lipp is about two Euros. Or as people remember it fondly,* many a drop is schlip between the pennig and the lipp.

'Do pirates come this far inland?' Cybelle held up a necklace with a delicate anchor-shaped charm at the clasp. The anchor spun back and forth, catching the light. Strange that the main feature of the necklace should be at the back, until Ondine realised it was designed to be worn with your hair up.

Marguerite stepped closer to admire the booty. 'Do we invoke the international treaty of "finders keepers"?'

Unable to stop herself, Ondine reached forwards and picked up a couple of elegant necklaces. One looked as delicate and complicated as a crocheted doily, if you could make a doily from spun silver then BeDazzle[31] it with diamonds.

Ma sounded out of breath. 'Let's just think about this for a minute. Think about where all of this may have come from.'

Ondine could have sworn she saw a gob of spittle dart from her mother's mouth, as if she were salivating over their new-found riches. Nobody else took any

---

31 *A completely unnecessary yet strangely compelling device to attach sparkly plastic jewels to your clothes.*

notice of her – they were all too busy making strange 'ooh' noises and admiring piece after piece.

'Let's move it to the back room for the moment, so we can keep working on the clean-up,' Ma said at last.

'Er, no, my love, I think this means work stops for the day,' Da said, rubbing his hand over his chin in thought.

'Have ye all lawst yer minds?' Shambles said, climbing Ondine's shoulder. 'There's a halth inspecta coming.'

Ondine shook her head to try and grab hold of her senses again. 'Um, everyone, Shambles just made a good point: we need to hide the loot from the health inspector.' She too found herself caught in the web of admiration. The next object she picked up was a simple bracelet made from braided gold. She couldn't help testing the latch to see if it would fit around her wrist.

'Stop thinking how good it looks on ye,' Shambles warned.

With reluctance she put the fine piece back in the box.

Ma took a deep breath and stepped back. 'Chef,

Thomas, Josef, get that box out the back somewhere safe. We'll keep going with the cleaning up in here.'

A heavy creak of timber provided an immediate stop to the discussion, as the front door pushed open to reveal a suit-clad woman (and not the man they'd been expecting) holding a clipboard. A pair of soda-bottle thick, tortoiseshell-rimmed glasses sat on the bridge of her thin nose, making her deep grey eyes appear much larger than they should.

In a flurry of movement, everyone tossed their jewels into the box. The men made themselves look busy. Ma and her daughters stood in front of the box to hide it.

Something about the woman looked odd to Ondine. It wasn't her short, salt-and-pepper hair or her enormously wide bottom and thighs, barely reined in by her too-tight skirt, although that did look weird. For a moment longer Ondine found herself staring, before she worked it out. The woman had no eyelashes at all.

'Quick, make a distraction,' Shambles ordered.

Extending her hand in greeting, Ondine walked

towards their visitor. 'Hello, you must be the health inspector. My name's Ondine and I've just come back from Psychic Summercamp. May I please read your palm? Oh, thank you,' she said, taking the woman's hand before she had time to refuse. All the while, Ondine's heart hammered behind her ribs, shocked at her own audaciousness.

'You have a rodent on your shoulder,' the woman said, her eyelash-less eyes widening even more.

'Grrrrr,' Shambles said.

Lurch went Ondine's stomach. Perhaps the ferret on the shoulder wasn't such a good idea, hygiene-wise? 'Oh please, pay him no mind – he's my familiar, and he's also my assignment from Summercamp. And he's a ferret, not a rodent. Member of the stoat and otter family; completely different species to rodents. They're very clean animals, ferrets. Can't speak for rats or mice though. Well, look here at your life line.' Ondine channelled her mother's skill of jumping from one subject to the next without pausing for breath.

It wasn't a case of seeing anything in the palm, because Ondine didn't have a clue what to look for.

It didn't matter – all she had to do was distract the woman, not divine her future. Which meant saying the the first thing that popped into her head.

'You have three grown sons. The youngest is a teenager who is still at school, but the other two are older and have careers now.'

'How did you know that?' the woman said, her steely grey eyes softening at the information. She still hadn't introduced herself, but that opportunity seemed to have passed.

Keep going, that's the best diversion.

'You don't like what the eldest is doing. It's not that you disapprove, it's just that you worry about him. He is really happy because he's following his dream. The middle son is a bit of a plodder. He's good, but he's coasting along, isn't he? You know he can do better but he won't apply himself. The youngest is your baby, and always will be, but you need to let him grow up and make his own mistakes.'

'Well, I'll be!' the woman said. 'If you tell me what my name is then I'll really believe you're psychic.'

Something tingled inside Ondine, a mixture of full-blown pride at her success so far and adrenalin at how daring she had become. 'It's Wilma Klegg, but that doesn't make me psychic, merely observant. It's written on the top of your clipboard.' A smile of satisfaction spread over her face. A buzz of confidence filled her soul.

Hey, I can do this.

'Ondine, please leave the health inspector alone, she has a job to do,' Ma said as she approached them. Her mother's voice sounded annoyed and imperious. To an outsider, it would seem like the mother was rescuing a visitor from a precocious child. However, the de Groot women knew Ondine had just saved them a whole heap of trouble.

As Ma led Mrs Klegg towards the kitchen, she turned back to Ondine and mouthed the words, 'Thank you.'

'Ye did well, lass. That was inspired, like.' Shambles gave her a wet, whiskery kiss on the cheek. 'I'm really proud of ye.'

A little thrill of excitement raced through Ondine. 'I just said whatever popped into my head. I guessed she had kids, because you don't get thighs like that on a spinster. I took her right hand, and I saw the ring on it, with three sapphires, so I figured that she'd had three boys.'

'Eh? Jewellery marks children?'

Ondine beamed. Who'd have thought she'd enjoy pretending to be psychic? 'Why yes, Shambles. When a woman gives birth, the very least her devoted husband can do is to shower her in jewellery to mark the occasion. It's a very strong tradition in my family. Haven't you seen my ma's rings, with the rubies set in them? One ruby for each of us.'

'Top marks for being observant. But what about all that guff about her boys and how she treats them?'

A chuckle escaped Ondine's lips as she bent down to the floor to scoop up mouldy newspapers for the fire, checking them first in case they contained anything juicy about the former Duke. 'I just thought about the way Da thinks of us. I think I'm starting to work out why he's so strict with me. I'm his baby; he doesn't want me growing up too soon. When the first child leaves the nest, the parents fall over themselves with worry. I just figured that if Mrs Klegg had three boys, and we're three girls, how different can it be? I just told her what she wanted to hear.'

'Well then, yer truly psychic. The old lady Howser would be proud of ye.'

'Mrs Howser?' Ondine thought of her Psychic Summercamp instructor. 'I bet she hasn't even noticed I'm gone.'

With a pang she thought of her friend Melody, and how much she missed her.

'Did I ever tell ye how I came to be at Mrs Howser's?' Shambles asked.

'I don't believe you have,' Ondine said, not really paying him much attention because she felt too nervous about what the health inspector might find.

'It's a funny story, really. After Old Col cast her spell I was all adrift, ye might say. She was friends with Mrs Howser at the time, ye see. But they weren't really friends because they weren't very nice to each other. More what you call *frenemies*. Are ye even listening to me, Ondi?'

What? 'Yes, of course.' Ondine watched Mrs Klegg and Ma disappear into the kitchens and heard lots of 'tisking' noises of disapproval.

'I never did meet Mr Howser. I don't think he lasted the distance. But Mrs Howser took a shine to me and stole me right from under Colette Romano's nose. I thought Colette would come for me, once she got over her fit of pique, but she never did.'

'That's nice,' Ondine said, barely hearing a word of it.

An hour later, Wilma Klegg's scowl deepened into a dark furrow. The more her lips thinned and pressed together like closed book pages, the more Ma's painted-on smile looked ready to crack. Wilma pulled on her white gloves and ran her finger over the kitchen benches. She sighed with disappointment. Something heavy fell in Ondine's stomach. A sense of foreboding clamped around her heart.

'We are closed for renovations, so it's natural the building is not up to correct specifications,' Ma explained, her hands clasped in front of her stomach so that just her thumbs had room to wriggle – which they did, putting the world's best fidget to shame. 'Furnish us with a list and we'll comply with everything on it.'

'Yes, you will,' Mrs Klegg said.

'It's all mince,'[32] Shambles said from Ondine's shoulder. They were both watching from a safe distance. 'The Duke would run ye out of town, so he would. More than likely that box of bangles under the floor is at the centre of it all.'

An idea percolated in Ondine's mind, so she re-read the newspaper obituary about the Duke's father and made a note of the newspaper's date.

'I reckon those jewels are the old Duke's secret stash,' Shambles said.

Ondine wondered if her parents were thinking along the same lines. 'Maybe you're right about the Duke, Shambles,' Ondine said, although she found it very hard to believe Vincent had anything to do with

---

32 *a) Something that looks good at first but turns out to be horrible, or just plain rubbish.*

  b) Used to make sausages.

this. 'Let's go to the city library and see if we can find out more.' She grabbed her tattered school bag and headed for the door.

The warm sun and fresh air cleared the dust from Ondine's brain as she walked to the train station. Shambles clung to her shoulder. She might not be able to help the family any further with the health inspector, but if she could find some more information about the former Duke, it might give them a way to get the present Duke off their case.

'Yer a good lass, and I like the view from here,' Shambles said with a saucy chuckle. Blushing furiously, Ondine looked down to see his point of view – the open 'V' in the neck of her shirt. The day felt hot already, but she quickly did all her buttons up. Would there be no end to this blushing?

To think I actually missed you!

The ancient bluestone building frightened Ondine at first. It was so tall and dark and it blocked out the sun. Her legs felt a little wobbly as she scaled the steps. With the ferret moving about on her shoulder, she felt sure someone would stop her at the door.

'Keep still,' she whispered to him, but it was no use.

A librarian approached, looked a bit startled, then settled his features and gave Ondine a smile that made his eyes crinkle all the way to his temples. 'You'll find pet care and animals in 636. It's the second row on the right.'

'Thank you, but I'm not here for that. I'd like to look at some newspapers from thirty years ago, please. Where would they be?'

'They're in the archive room, but you won't be able to take animals in there, I'm afraid. It's a controlled environment.'

'Um, what about if I sat outside the archive room, and you brought the papers to me? Would that be OK?'

'Good thinking, lass,' Shambles whispered.

The librarian shook his head. 'I'm sorry, we can't do that either. Have you got a box you could put your pet in for the time being? Otherwise you could put her in a locker.'

'I'll naw go in a box!' Shambles protested, but it fell on deaf ears as Ondine accepted the compromise and took a locker key. He didn't bother protesting at being mistaken for a girl. Ondine felt no compulsion to correct the librarian, because she didn't want him paying any closer attention to her 'pet' passenger.

'Hush up. It's for your own good.' A tingle of delight raced up Ondine's spine. She was enjoying this.

'Dinnae put me in the locker!' he pleaded, as she opened the ventilated door.

'Stop whining. Just pretend you're going in, then at the last second get in my bag and stay absolutely still.'

Shambles had the choice – shut in a metal box or crammed into the bag. He chose the latter and kept quiet.

The archive room smelt of naphthalene,[33] making Ondine's eyes water and the inside of her nose freeze. Shafts of light poured through from the small windows up on high, giving the room an ethereal feel. She found the pile of newspapers and worked backwards from the date of the old Duke's obituary, scanning for

---

33 *Magnificent compound for preventing moths and silverfish from eating your clothes. However, the smell is almost impossible to eradicate, which explains why your nana smells like that.*

anything mentioning his name. In the months prior to his death, she found a page of court reports, and one short item that outlined a failed criminal case against the old Duke. There were lots of quotes from the old Duke's lawyer saying they were 'always confident the unconstitutional charges would be dropped'. Hope and a little bit of confusion surged in Ondine's chest. They were on to something.

'Turning the pages back in time, they found an earlier court report.

'It says here the lawyers for the Duke are challenging the "constitutional validity" of the charges. Can you make sense of this?'

Shambles peered at the newsprint, his head turning left and right as he scanned the column of text. 'Aye, he's saying he can't be brought to trial because he's the Duke. They're quoting the ancient law of *nascut regulum*.'[34]

'What's that supposed to mean?'

'I don't know, but it worked.'

Turning the pages yet further back in time, they

---

34 *Ancient Brugler-Latin for 'born to rule'.*

found few mentions of the Duke, apart from the regular fortnightly list of visiting dignitaries. Almost as if the newspaper was pointedly ignoring him.

But of course, they were looking at this with hindsight – nobody at the time knew he was about to pop his clogs. For a while Ondine became distracted with other news events, and all the photographs highlighting the bizarre fashions of the day made her snort.

Then something caught her eye – a photograph of the old Duke and Duchess at an opening night at the theatre. The Duchess was wearing a diamond necklace that at first looked like a triangle of lace. Ondine got out her notepad and drew a picture of the necklace and the rest of the jewellery the Duchess wore. It was an old photograph, and although Ondine was no jewellery designer, she felt sure she'd seen that same piece in the box they'd uncovered under her family's floorboards.

'Eh, lass, didya read the rest of it?' Shambles said. 'Says here the Duchess's jewellery is on loan from the Hera Collection. Have you heard of them?'

'Nope, can't say I have. Stay quiet and I'll get the

librarian to help me look it up.' Before Shambles could protest, she shoved him back into her bag.

That old familiar, tingling feeling of excitement started to course through her veins. Ondine knew she was on to something, and it felt great. Now to find the librarian and gather more information.

To Ondine's surprise, her questions weren't something the man had to look up. He'd heard of the Hera Collection before, and knew where the best book on the subject could be found.

'It's famous, but a bit before your time,' he said, reaching for an enormous book filled with colour-plate images of some of the finest jewellery Ondine had ever seen.

'Have a look at these and try to keep your eyes in your head,' the librarian added.

Drooling in a public library was not the done thing, so Ondine kept her mouth closed and swallowed several times in an effort to stop salivating. Page after page of incredible designs made her want to weep. There were clusters of choker necklaces, strings of pearls, glistening tiaras and stunning multi-jewelled earrings with matching necklaces. There were delicate rings for young debutantes, along with gaudy big monsters for fat old ladies with chubby fingers.

When she turned the page her breath hitched in her throat. It was a picture of the same necklace the Duchess had worn in the old newspaper photo. Ondine put the picture she'd sketched beside the photograph and her heart started beating way too fast at the discovery. Then she took out her pencil and altered her drawing, rubbing a bit out here and there, sketching it again, and so on, until her drawing was perfect.

Look, she had a good brain, but she just didn't have the artistic bent Marguerite possessed, so the drawing and re-drawing took a while.[35]

Eventually, she was done. 'Thank you so much for

---

35 *You may be wondering why Ondine didn't just get on the Internet and look this up. Truth be told, Brugel is the only country in Europe without broadband. They also have high tariffs on imported computers, to encourage people to 'Buy Brugel Made'.*

Their phone system is prone to outages as well, which is why they still have a voting panel for the Eurovision Song Contest instead of phone and SMS voting. Brugel always gives twelve points to Slovakia, which has led to accusations of vote-rigging. Especially when Slovakia wasn't even in the finals last year.

your help,' Ondine said to the librarian as she packed her things and shoved them into her bag. A muffled 'ooof' sounded from inside it, but she coughed to smother Shambles's grunts.

She couldn't get home fast enough with the exciting news.

'Ondi, thank goodness for your perception,' Ma said when Ondine returned home, Shambles riding high on her shoulder. 'Mrs Klegg would have seen that entire box of jewels if you hadn't acted as fast as you did. And your psychic gift kicked in at just the right time. She was really very impressed with your vision, which made up for what she saw around here. Look at this: she's given us a list of repairs and changes to make, and then we can re-open next week.'

But I was guessing, Ondine wanted to say, but she held her thoughts for a moment so she could explain what she'd learned in the library. 'I need to see the jewellery. Ma, have you heard of the Hera Collection?'

'The Hera Collection? Of course I have, every woman's heard of it.'

'Well, I hadn't. Until today, that is,' Ondine protested.

'It was before your time, dear,' Ma said.

A disappointed sigh escaped Ondine. Why did older people have to be so patronising about things and events taking place 'before their time'? That complaint would have to wait until another day though – right now she had more pressing matters.

'The Duke. The one before the one we've got. Shambles and I have been to the library, and we've got the goods on him. The old Duchess borrowed pieces from the Hera Collection. One of them looks like this,' Ondine said, showing her mother the drawing she'd made of the necklace.

They didn't waste any time heading to Ma and Da's bedroom, where they found Cybelle and Marguerite sitting on the bed, trying on jewels and giggling like toddlers.

'Margi, stand up now,' Ma commanded.

The eldest obeyed, her eyes downcast in shame at their discovery. The glittering jewels on her neck practically danced in the sunlight.

Excitement bubbled in Ondine and she beamed with pride as she took in the delicate necklace around her sister's neck.

'It's the same one all right,' Shambles said. 'Looks good on her, too.'

Chapter Eight

A few days later, Ondine was none the wiser about the jewels.

'Tell me again why the Hera Collection won't go public?' Ondine asked her mother as they set about rolling out the new carpet for the dining room.

It had been a crazy time. In the last week Ma had taken it upon herself to make contact with the Hera Collection and organise the safe return of the jewels. The cash, on the other hand? Nobody needed to know about that, so it found its way into the deposit box under the kitchen floor.

'They didn't want to go public because the old Duke and Duchess are no longer with us, and the present Duke's family is one of their best customers,' Ma declared.

'Haaalp!' Shambles yelled as he fell over backwards under the carpet roll.

'But the Duke stole from them, or at least, his dad did,' Ondine said as she grabbed Shambles out of harm's way. A good thing she'd acted so quickly, otherwise he would have ended his days as a nasty lump under the new carpet.

Only a few metres of carpet to go and they'd be finished. In this room at least.

'That's very true,' said Ma. 'But the present Duchess is photographed wearing their jewels, just as the old Duchess was, and by doing that she becomes a walking advertisement for them. They still make their money. We've spared them a public scandal.'

'Did they let us keep *any* of it as a reward?' Cybelle asked, hammering the carpet tacks into the corners of the room to keep the new flooring steady. 'Surely not all of it was theirs?'

'Surely it was,' Ma said, adding a heavy sigh for emphasis.

Tears pricked the back of Ondine's eyes. All that

beautiful jewellery, gone just as fast as it had come into their lives.

'But that's not fair! They could have left us some of it, as thanks for saving their reputation,' Marguerite complained as she and Thomas moved another table into position. Despite the hard work, Marguerite's long dark hair looked glossy and wavy. Cybelle's bob looked neat and tidy. Ondine? Her hair hung in messy string-tails and the top of her scalp felt greasy.

'I'm afraid not. They couldn't risk somebody recognising the pieces on any of us. Imagine if we wore them to a public event. We'd be in jail for theft faster than you could say "that's not fair".'

'Because we're not the kind of people who are allowed to wear it. Are we?' Ondine said, clenching her hands in frustration.

That's all life seemed to be lately. One frustrating event after another.

'But why did you have to give it *all* back then?' Cybelle moaned, doing a very good job of sounding coherent considering that she had a dozen carpet tacks in her mouth.

'Pfft! I didn't give it *all* back. D'you think I'm stupid?' Ma said, then sat back and had a good chuckle at her daughters' expense.

Anger and jubilation roiled in Ondine. Anger that their mother had told them a whopping great fib. Jubilation that there were still a few nice pieces somewhere in safe keeping.

'You were winding us up, weren't you, Ma?' Ondine finished rolling the carpet out. Then she trimmed off the extra length with a sharp knife. A few more tacks from Cybelle and they'd be done for the afternoon. Not much left on Mrs Klegg's list now.

In unison, Marguerite and Cybelle rolled their eyes in frustration. Getting a straight answer out of their mother would be impossible now, because Ma knew how much they'd wanted to keep some of those trinkets and baubles for themselves.

'On to important business,' Da said as he entered the room. He and Chef manoeuvred the piano into its corner in the dining room. Everyone moved out the way to let them get it into place. Shambles leapt to the top of Ondine's shoulder.

Ma brushed down her skirts. 'We re-open tomorrow for lunch. I'm thinking perhaps with the new opening, we could give the place a new name.'

'What's wrong with the old one, Mrs G?' Thomas asked.

'Nyeh, it's too dull,' Ma said. 'It doesn't do anything for me any more. What do you think, Josef?'

'I think the present name is fine,' said Da. 'Everyone knows where *The Station Hotel* is – it's across the road from the station.'

'How about *The Jewel?*' Cybelle said with a wicked gleam in her eye.

'Or *The Crown?*' Marguerite said.

'I know. What if we call it *The Duke and Ferret?*' Ondine said.

They all laughed at that.

'You know what? That has a pretty good ring to it,' Ma said. 'And it could prove a handy insurance policy. The Duke wouldn't dare close down a pub named in his honour. Good thinking, Ondi. You truly have the gift.'

With that, her mother kissed her affectionately on

the forehead and surveyed the improvements. 'It all looks grand. Well done, everyone.'

Later that night, Ondine tried to sleep, but her brain would not switch off. Back in her own room again, she had no one to talk to. She took a walk down the darkened hall to see if Cybelle was awake. Judging from the rollicking snores, her sister was deeply out of it.

There was nothing for it but to chat with Shambles, simply because he would be up for a natter when nobody else would. But where was he? The kitchen seemed the logical place, and indeed, that was where she found him, licking cold fat off a dirty frying pan.

'Ye've come to take me to bed, lass?'

Did he have to be so cheeky all the time?

'You should be in the laundry. Everyone else is asleep.'

'So why are you up?'

A heavy weight pushed her shoulders down. 'It's Ma. I'm trying to work out how to tell her I don't have the *gift*.'

'Sure you've got the gift, so you do,' Shambles said.

Maybe some warm milk would help. Ondine set about making herself something comforting.

The drinking chocolate's around here somewhere.

'I don't have the gift,' she protested, her head starting to throb with confusion. It wasn't right to mislead her mother. If Ma got the idea into her head that Ondine really was psychic, she might send her youngest back to Summercamp and Mrs Howser. 'I've just been saying the first thing that comes into my head. That's not being psychic, it's just blurting things out. Most of the time without even thinking.'

'But they're the *right* things, so they are,' Shambles said.

Frustration made Ondine clench her teeth, but she resisted the urge to grind her back molars into powder. 'Well, maybe I'm just really smart. I mean, is that so far-fetched? Why does it have to be some extra power? Why can't I be the smart one instead of the psychic one?'

'It really bothers you, doesn't it, lass?'

Taking a few breaths, Ondine sorted her thoughts out. Too right it bothered her, for more reasons than she could say. Perhaps because the entire psychic concept left her feeling like a liar and a scam artist. She knew plenty of people who had the gift for real, but she wasn't one of them. And another thing. If people said she was psychic, they'd want more of it, and eventually it would all unravel because they'd find out there was no more to give. They'd find out she was a fraud.

It didn't feel right to foster a lie.

'You're a smart girl. You'll work it out,' Shambles said.

There was no time to think about anything the next morning, as the entire family – which now encompassed Thomas – set about readying for the lunchtime re-opening. Chef and Cybelle were little more than a blur of work in the kitchen; Thomas and Da polished the new beer glasses and steins; Margi, Ondine, Shambles and Ma made up the guests' beds on the second floor.

In a flash of black, Shambles darted under the bed they were working on.

'You've run under every bed up here. I didn't put

the jewels anywhere you could find them, you know,'
Ma said.

'I'm checking for Oose.[36] They breed under beds
and frighten folk.'

Ahead of her mother's question, Ondine shrugged.
'I have no idea what he's on about.'

'You knew what I was going to ask? I told you,
you're psychic,' Colette said.

A muscle twitched in Ondine's jaw. 'Ma, please.
Drop it, OK?'

'We're done here,' Marguerite interrupted. Apart
from the soft red in her cheeks, she still looked neat.
You'd never know she'd been doing so much work.
'We'd better get downstairs before the doors open, or
we'll be overrun.'

'Thank you, Margi, that's very *smart* of you,' Ondine
said with deliberate emphasis. Then she looked at her
mother. 'Or maybe Margi's the psychic one?'

---

36 *Mighty big clumps of dust that gang up into fluff monsters. The origin
of this phrase is impossible to verify, much like a Freemason's secret
handshake. For more information on Freemasonry, follow the adventures
of Pierre in Tolstoy's* War and Peace. *Or check out* Freemasons for
Dummies.

'You'll keep,' Ma said.

They made it down the stairs just in time to see Thomas open the door to half a dozen thirsty people, who made straight for the bar and ordered drinks. In a couple of seconds Da had his hands full of beer steins and the till started ringing with sales. Cybelle walked into the bar carrying a plate of savoury morsels, offering them around.

'You're not giving food away, are you?' Ma whispered to her middle child.

'They're samples, Ma, as a re-opening special. It's Chef's idea. Isn't he clever? He has some really good ideas to update the menu and –'

'Right, I'll have a good talk to Chef.'

From her position in the doorway Ondine watched the exchange, and her heart ached for her middle sister. If she were older, she could walk into the bar and offered her moral support. Being only fifteen, she didn't dare set foot in it, just in case someone dobbed her in to the Duke or Mrs Klegg. Instead, she waited until she caught Cybelle's attention and gave her the thumbs-up, because that was all she could do for now.

Cybelle shot her back a confused look.

So much for being psychic.

The lunch crowd kept them busy all afternoon. The kitchen roared back into life with a host of new and delightful smells, courtesy of Chef's additions. Lunchtime grew into late afternoon and another of Chef's ideas – afternoon tea – brought in more people for scones, jam and cream, with tea or coffee. This time, Ma beamed at Chef's innovation, because it created a profitable time of the day where previously none had existed. And nobody needed free samples.

As Ondine served tea and scones to the guests, Cybelle took to the piano and Marguerite joined her. From out the back, Shambles raced through the dining room and scurried up on top of the piano to join in. Ondine held her breath, waiting for calamity, but this time nobody screamed. The girls laughed as the animal wailed and carried on, holding his little ferrety paws over his chest as he squeaked his heart out.

It had been an excellent idea renaming the place *The Duke and Ferret.* If anyone saw Shambles, they'd know he was the hotel mascot and not a rat.

Above the melody, Ondine heard the chink and clunk of coins piling into the tips jar on top of the piano. A beaming smile cracked her face.

This is brilliant!

'Shy little thing, isn't he?' Ma joked, then she too started singing on her way back to the kitchen, her arms full of dirty plates.

'He just wants to get out of work,' Ondine said. With a sigh she bade the piano farewell and made for the pile of dirty plates by the sink. She pushed her sleeves up and plunged her arms into the hot, soapy water.

Late afternoon rolled into early evening. Ondine sat in the private room behind the kitchen with Shambles, Cybelle and Chef. They were eating from a platter of food Chef had brought out for them, resting and recharging before the evening crowd arrived. As far as Ondine was concerned, Shambles had done the least real work out of the lot of them, but that didn't stop him eating his bodyweight in cold meats and cheeses.

'Born and bred salad dodger, aren't you, Shambles?' Chef said.

'I used to love potatoes and fresh fruit, but I cannae handle it no more,'[37] Shambles confessed, talking with his mouth full.

'You probably used to love table manners too,' Ondine said. Cybelle made a large 'O' with her mouth and re-applied her eyeliner.

Through the sound of munching and slurping water, Ondine heard her mother's voice rise an octave in delight, all the way from the dining room.

'Sounds like someone's turned up for Margi's engagement party tomorrow,' Cybelle said, as they heard their mother's voice grow louder on approach.

'It's lovely to see you again. Come through. Oh, you must see the girls, they've grown so much,' Ma said as she walked towards them.

There in the doorway stood Great Auntie Col.

Food dropped from Shambles's mouth. 'It's the witch! It's really her this time!' he shrieked.

---

37 *Ferrets are famous salad dodgers, and are unable to process sugars or even vegetable protein. Don't feed them raisins, as ferrets are also known to hoard their food. The sugar rush from a raisin bender can put them in a coma. Likewise with alcohol, but that's just common sense.*

Nobody said anything for what felt like ages, but in reality was probably only five seconds, as the elderly but sprightly woman creased her eyes and scrutinised Shambles.

A tiny bit of sick burnt the back of Ondine's throat, such was her shock and surprise. Old Auntie Col was here, the Witchy Woman who'd turned Hamish the lad into the animal he was today. Ondine swallowed hard and stared up at her elderly relative, her heart beating faster in anticipation of what might come.

'Hamish McPhee, you haven't changed a bit,' Auntie Col said.

'Aye, ye cursed me good, so ye did.'

'Not one of my better ones, but it seems to have stuck.'

'Aye. Come here and give me a kiss.' Shambles held his furry arms wide for a hug.

A cold spike of jealousy stabbed Ondine's heart. What if Auntie Col returned Shambles to his Hamish-ness, and he up and left them?

Another cold spike, this time of fear. What if it was even worse? What if Auntie Col returned

Shambles to his Hamish-ness, and he was *ugly*?

Don't be so superficial.

But once the thought took hold, she couldn't stop it.

Chapter Nine

They'd been talking for more than two hours, Shambles and Old Aunt Col, but Ondine had no idea what they were talking about. Every time she returned from the dining room with empty plates, she looked in on the private room behind the kitchen. There they were, Shambles jittering about on the table and Old Col nodding her head from time to time. They spoke in hushed tones, their backs to the doorway so Ondine couldn't even read their expressions.

The old lady and the ferret. What *could* they be talking about?

'No slacking off, go take table twelve's dessert order,' Ma said. 'Leave Hamish and Aunt Col alone. When they're ready to talk to you, they'll let you know.'

A spark raced up Ondine's spine. Her mother

had called him Hamish instead of Shambles. Would that mean her great-aunt had decided to release the enchantment so he could become human again? Yet again Ondine wondered whether Hamish might be as handsome as he sounded. Or at the very least, as handsome as Lord Vincent.

I shouldn't compare them, but I can't help it.

It was impossible for Hamish to sit still. Being a human with ferret qualities (although by now perhaps it was the other way around) he did his best to listen quietly and 'sit nice'[38] as his mother used to say. It was a losing battle. The mixture of excitement and fear coursing through his body had him trembling from nose to tail-tip.

'Ye understand how completely sorry I am,' he started, knowing it barely touched the sides of the cavernously bad feeling existing between them.

'You offended me mightily, you know that,' Aunt

---

38 *Sit Nice. Instruction for children to behave, used sparingly if at all, because of its negligible value in teaching children anything. More often used as a precursor to a smack. As in, 'I told ye tae sit nice and ye didnae. (Smack!) Now stop crying and go to your room.'*

Col said, and from the look on her face – as wrinkly and 'of a certain age' as it was – she'd kept hold of her pain for many, many years.

'Aye, I know, and I am deeply sorry. And at first I was angry with ye for doin' it, but I've come to understand why ye did it. Ye've taught me a lesson, one I'll nawt likely forget,' Hamish said, taking a deep breath (for a ferret anyway) and trying to move the conversation forwards. 'I didn't realise yer debutante ball was so important to ye. But I know I ruined it for ye, and I'm very sorry. If you change me back, I'll partner ye again and we'll get it right this time.'

They both sat there for a moment, as Hamish looked at Old Col, and she looked back at him. All the while Hamish's tiny heart whirred like a drum roll.

'Eh, lass? Now that we're older and wiser, is there any chance ye can forgive me?'

The papery skin on Old Col's face made a concertina on her cheeks as she smiled. 'You're half right. I'm certainly much older, and I do believe I am somewhat wiser. You did hurt me, Hamish, for many reasons – but you're right, it was a long time ago, and holding a grudge is so terribly ageing.'

Hamish held his breath, waiting for the next bit.

'I forgive you,' Old Col said, her eyes sparkling behind their stubby lashes.

In those few words, Hamish felt his spirits soar. Then just as quickly they crashed as he surveyed his furry body. 'But, I'm still a ferret!'

'So you are. Which means it's up to you now. Perhaps you like being a ferret because it means you are excused from life's obligations.'

'So you're saying I'm still a ferret because . . . because I *like* it?'

The grin she gave him sent a heavy, sinking feeling into the pit of his stomach.

'That must be it. Weasel your way out of that one!'

The minutes dragged like hours, until towards the end of the evening, Ondine finally heard Old Aunt Col summon her to sit beside them at their table. The wrinkles on her face and her gnarled, arthritic fingers may have given the woman an appearance of age, but her mind still cracked as fast as a whip.

'Ondine, come here, child. Hamish has something he wishes to say to you,' Aunt Col said, motioning to the ferret, who sat near the edge of the table with his head bowed.

'Aye, lass, I do. But before I go on, I want to tell ye how much I appreciate everything ye've done for me. Ye've taken me in and provided for me. I couldnae asked for more.'

Fear gripped Ondine's heart and gave a good squeeze. His words sounded so ominous. Her hands wobbled, so she clasped them together to hold them still.

'Aunt Col has lifted the spell, but I think I've been a ferret so long I've forgotten what I used to be. She says it's up to me now, but I'm nawt sure I know how to be me again. Ye've shown me what it means to be part of a family, to work together and make a real go of it.'

Ondine pleaded with Aunt Col. 'Change him back!'

'I already have. He's responsible for his life now.'

'But you turned him into a ferret in the first place,' Ondine protested.

'That's true, but spells only work on willing

recipients. I did call him a weasel for being so horrible
to me and ruining my big night, but he must have
believed it to make the spell work.'

'So why isn't he changing back then?'

A sad little voice piped up, 'Because ah'm nawt
worthy of ye.'

Ondine noted the drawl in his accent, proving
just how deeply embarrassed he felt. 'Don't be
silly. Of course you're worthy. You're helping out
around the pub and you prevented the Duke's
assassination, for goodness' sake. They're pretty worthy
things in my book.'

The little ferret gave a sigh and said, 'Yeah, I
guess so.'

But he didn't sound convinced.

A tear trickled down Ondine's cheek at the thought
of Hamish living the rest of his life trapped in that
little body.

'Ach, dry yer eyes,'[39] Shambles said, his accent

---

39 *Often spoken in comfort, but just as often not, depending on tone, e.g.*
'Oh, did ye drop yer wee bottle of ginger and it's all splished away? Ach,
dry yer eyes.'

Compared to: 'Ye fell out the windae and got a compound fracture?

sounding even thicker with remorse. 'Ah know ye were looken forward to me being human again, but ye'll have to wait a bit until I get mah heed right.'

Now who's the psychic one?

Later that night, when all was quiet, Shambles sneaked into Ondine's room. In automatic response to seeing the ferret near her bed, Ondine patted the pillow and made room for him.

'Nay, lass, I just came to bid you goodnight. Now get yer sleep. I'm for the laundry.'

A heavy feeling tugged at Ondine's heart. As if she were missing him already. 'You don't have to sleep down there, Shambles. Ma knows you're here anyway.'

'All the more reason to stay in the laundry. It's nawt appropriate for me to be in yer room. I've taken advantage of yer . . . *hospitality* . . . enough.'

Ondine heard the emphasis on the word and chose to ignore it. She opened her mouth to speak, but nothing came out because her mind had gone

---

Ach, dry yer eyes.' Closest modern equivalent is 'Suck it up and get back to work.'

blank.[40] Possibly because all she could do was imagine how lonely she'd be without him snuggled in beside her. For a while Ondine sat there in her bed, while Shambles stood there in the middle of the floor, neither saying anything for what felt like the longest time.

Finally, Shambles sighed. 'I think yer aunty's right. I have to behave like a man. I think mebbe if I go with her we might be able to find some spells that might help.'

He was leaving? How would that help anyone?

'Sham– no, Hamish?' Ondine cleared her throat. 'You're the only one here who doesn't treat me like a child. Please don't start now.'

'Yer nawt a child, that's for sure.' The ferret shook his furry head. 'You're the smartest one here. And that's why I have tae go. I'll only drag ye down if I remain.'

Nothing he said made any sense. 'You'll at least stay for Margi's party tomorrow night, won't you?' Ondine tried to sound reasonable, while in her heart she felt very close to begging. Only she wouldn't beg, and she

---

40 *Not completely blank, obviously, otherwise her vital functions like breathing would stop. But the thinking part of her brain shut down.*

wouldn't whine, because that would betray how mature she was trying to appear.

'One last party, eh? Well, OK, if it means that much to ye.'

Ondine's shoulders sagged in relief. She hadn't realised how tense she'd become during the course of their conversation, but now she sighed out loud with the reprieve. Maybe she could convince Aunt Col and Shambles to stay with them? After all, they had room for plenty more under their roof.

Shambles made for the door, but stopped before he left.

'Is there something else?' Ondine asked.

'Yeah, there is. Yer ma told me about Lord Vincent. She said he was making puppy eyes at you in the dining room the other day.'

'Thanks, Ma.' Ondine flushed.

Shambles shrugged. 'Big families are short on privacy.'

'What about Lord Vincent?' she asked, as a fresh wave of tingling spread across her wrist at the memory of his kiss.

'You're a smart girl. I think you already know.'

'And if I wasn't smart? If I was only a child. What would you tell me?'

'I'd tell you to stay away from him, because he reminds me too much of me.'

With that, Shambles walked out of her room, leaving Ondine with a sinking, empty feeling inside.

That night, as Ondine slept, she tried to dream of Lord Vincent, but her subconscious wouldn't let her. Instead, Melody, her friend from Psychic Summercamp, appeared. *Pang!* Ondine had meant to keep in touch with her friend, but things had become so busy she hadn't found the time. In the dream, they were sitting in a field of flowers, at dusk on a balmy summer's evening. Fireflies danced around them. It was a lovely, calm scene, and Shambles appeared (eating a sausage, of course, because any time Ondine thought of Shambles it was associated with eating). It all felt so peaceful, Ondine wanted the dream to last for ages.

'Mrs Howser wants to see you,' Melody said.

Her friend's words brought a change of scene.

It became dark and a cold draught played around her legs, yet a bright spotlight shone on her. Shambles stopped eating and cried out in pain, clutching his belly.

'We're coming,' Melody said.

'I'm dying,' Shambles said.

Ondine sprang awake, dripping with perspiration while her heart thundered behind her ribs, threatening to burst free.

'I'm not psychic, it was just a dream,' she said to the empty room.

So why couldn't she convince herself?

Not sleeping properly made Ondine grumpy. When Melody and Mrs Howser arrived in the dining room late the next afternoon, her heart sank and she became even grumpier. Not because she didn't like them, but the fact that they were here in person meant perhaps the rest of last night's dream might come true as well. The bit that didn't end well for Shambles. Still, she hugged Melody hello.

'Hey, Ondi, it's good to see you! Did you get my

message in your dream?' Melody beamed. 'I've cracked astral projection at last. Mrs Howser's been so helpful. Is Shambles still here?'

'Th-that was you?' Cold dread snaked through her system.

'Yes! I'm still not sure how much came through. I used a new technique, but I *was* in your dream last night, wasn't I? I can tell because you've gone pale. Oh dear, I didn't go overboard, did I?' Melody blurted.

Ondine wanted to be sick.

'Aren't you going to show us to a table?' Mrs Howser asked as she hitched a multitude of coloured shawls over her shoulders. High summer, but the woman acted like she had a chill. 'You can tell us how you're getting along with Shambles. I've actually missed him.'

Remembering her manners just in time (and taking a deep breath so she could rein in her nausea), Ondine invited them to take a seat, then dashed to the kitchen and returned a few minutes later with a pot of steaming tea.

'We're flat out, to tell the truth. We have a pretty full dining room tonight, and it's Margi's engagement party to Thomas after that. Hi, Thomas,' she added, as the topic of conversation walked in, bringing a decanter of wine to the patrons on a nearby table.

'I know it's your sister's engagement party,' Mrs Howser said with a haughty tone. 'Your mother invited us, in exchange for me graciously returning the remainder of your tuition fees. Even though I was under no obligation, due to you leaving in somewhat hurried circumstances.'

Gulp.

'Hey, Ondi. Thanks for stringing up the fairy lights in the garden – they'll look great in the dark,' Thomas said.

Ondine felt eternally grateful for Thomas's interjection. She was really starting to like her future brother-in-law, and felt a little glow of extra love for her eldest sister. Margi had chosen well.

Melody piped up, 'Fairy lights? But in the dream they were fireflies.'

Something staggered behind Ondine's ribs and her

throat turned to ash. Everything about her dream was coming true.

'Where is Shambles?' Mrs Howser asked.

'H-he's around here somewhere. He's fitting in really well,' Ondine said, making bland conversation while she tried to work out whether Melody and Mrs Howser appearing meant everything else in the dream would happen. The moment she had some free time, she'd take down those horrible fairy lights. Surely, if they weren't there, the rest of the dream couldn't come true?

At that point, Ma and Old Aunt Col came in. Ondine took the initiative and made introductions, pulling up more chairs to accommodate them, all the while trying to find an excuse to leave. As soon as she could get out to the garden, she could sabotage her earlier work.

'We've already met,' Aunt Col said, giving Mrs Howser a stern look. 'Been a while, Birgit. Still glomming round the camp, gazing at tea leaves?'

'Hello, Col. Still spitting acid, I see?'

It was physically impossible for Ondine's eyeballs

to pop out of her head, but it felt like they were about to, such was her shock. 'Um, Melody, why don't we go out to the beer garden and help with the decorations?'

If these two old biddies wanted to trade insults down memory lane, she'd rather not be around to see it.

'Oh, it's just like the dream!' Melody said with delight as she saw the lights strung up between the trees. In twilight, the effect wasn't very good, but when the sun set in a hour or so, they would look just like fireflies.

A heavy sense of dread choked Ondine's throat as she pulled up a chair and removed a strand of lights from the nearest tree branch. 'No, it's not! Melody, what did you do? I woke up and nearly puked, I was so sick with fear. Why did you put that bit in about Shambles dying?'

Now it was Melody's turn to go pale, leaving nothing but contrasting brown freckles on her face. 'But I didn't. We were in a field of fireflies and I said we were coming to pay a visit. Shambles wasn't even in it. He's not sick, is he?'

Confusion time. 'Are you sure?' Ondine rolled up the cables.

'Yes, absolutely positive, I promise,' Melody said.

Ondine took a few deep breaths to steady her nerves. There was no point even trying to think with all this adrenalin racing around her body. It made her tremble and want to cry and yet she felt strangely hungry all at the same time. She needed a clear head so she could think about a rational answer, not turn into an emotional wreck.

So Melody had not dreamt of Shambles? At last, a positive sign! Things were looking up. If all of Melody's side of the dream came true, no dramas there. Just as long as Shambles's part didn't come true.

'It's OK. I've got my wires crossed. Let's get the rest of this set up. We should keep busy out here so we can stay well clear of the two witches inside, don't you think?'

Melody giggled.

There were tablecloths and piles of plates and cutlery to set out for that night's party, so they set to it.[41] Ma had planned the evening to coincide with the full moon, so they'd have plenty of natural light to add to the mood. Work proved a welcome distraction, and before long they had the place looking very inviting.

'Ondi, maybe . . . maybe I crashed the dream you were already having,' Melody suggested as she placed knives and forks at each setting.

'Yeah, that could work. I mean, hey, it was just a dream, right?'

'Well, of course. Sometimes a dream is just a dream. It doesn't have to mean anything,' Melody said.

The object of their concern came bounding out into the beer garden in a streak of dark fur, his mouth full of food. 'Ondi, ye've got to try Chef's new meatballs, they're to die for,' Shambles said. Actually, what he really said was 'O-fi, oof ot oo iy eff's ew eetaaals, ere o ie or' because he had a mouth full of food.

---

41 It may seem short notice to be having the engagement party so soon after Josef discovered his eldest's intentions. However, just as Ma had kept a good secret from her husband about Margi and Thomas, she'd also kept the party secret, only telling Josef that morning that it was on. Her reasoning was that if she didn't tell him until the last minute, it would be too late to cancel it.

'Weh hey!' In a blaze of black fur, he leapt on to the top of the last un-set table and skidded along the surface, the tablecloth bunching up at his feet.

The girls laughed at Shambles, even though Ondine should have been cross with him. But she couldn't be, not when he might be leaving soon with Aunt Col. She wouldn't let them end things on an argument.

'Aw, I messed up yer table,' Shambles said, surveying the damage. 'I'll fix it up for ye.' With that, he gripped the edge of the fabric in his teeth and walked backwards across the surface, dragging the cloth with him.

From the other end, Ondine held the edges in place, smoothing it out and making it ready.

'Thanks, Shambles, you're a great help,' she said.

Suddenly, with a yelp of shock, the ferret dropped backwards off the edge of the table, dragging the tablecloth down with him.

'Shambles!' Ondine screamed, racing towards him.

He lay there, a lump underneath the fabric, moaning in pain.

'Oh, my darling, I'm so sorry!' Ondine cried. She didn't need to look around to know Melody was standing behind her. Ondine pulled the tablecloth back to reveal Shambles's head and give him some fresh air.

Shambles groaned even louder. 'Oh, the pain!'

'He can talk! Great heavens! Shambles can talk!' Melody said, amazed.

'You heard that?' Ondine's heart picked up speed at the revelation, yet there was little time to explain it all. If she thought Melody being able to understand Shambles was a shock, she had an even bigger one coming.

As he lay groaning and writhing on the ground, twisting and turning under the tablecloth, Shambles grew to twice his size and his face fur matted together, forming skin. The long whiskers retracted and his head began to bulge.

'I'm dying!' he cried out to Ondine. 'Bring me whisky, I'm dying!'

The dream. That horrible dream!

'Mercury's wings!' Ondine cried as great wet tears splashed down her face and on to Shambles's writhing, deformed body. 'You can't die, Shambles! I won't let you!'

'I'll get Mrs Howser,' Melody said, and ran back inside.

'Oh God, oh God,' Shambles groaned, 'I'm goin' tae boak.'[42]

'No, Shambles, you'll be OK. Melody's getting help,' Ondine said, although what help anyone could be at this present moment escaped her. On the other hand, a witch had got him into this mess; maybe a witch could get him out of it? Confusion scrambled her brain. She couldn't think what to do – she'd never seen anything like this before and didn't even know how to start helping him. All she could do was stand back as Shambles kept growing and expanding under the tablecloth. Moaning and groaning about the state of his gelatinous body. All the while his face pulsed and wobbled. A horrible thought made Ondine feel ashamed for even thinking it. What if his face set like that?

'There's the light,' he said, 'it's calling me, I have tae go tae the light.'

Fear making her tremble, Ondine looked in the

_____

42 *Vomit. A lot. Usually after drinking. A lot.*

same direction. Her horrible dream was about to become reality. As she turned her head, she felt her stomach lurch as a white light shone on her face. A moment later, blessed relief coursed all through her body. 'That's not the light, Shambles. That's just the full moon, you bampot.'

When she turned to check on Shambles, her breath hitched in her throat. He'd stopped thrashing about, stopped moaning and groaning. Now he was shivering.

And completely human.

The next surprise came straight after the first, as Shambles looked up at Ondine. Far from looking like a bucket of twisted shoes, his face could have belonged to a movie star. He was even more handsome than Lord Vincent. With a shock of black hair and a dangerous gleam in his green eyes.

And he was glorious.

Heat coursed through her body and her tongue turned to sandpaper as she tried to swallow. Something flip-flopped in her belly. Thank heavens for the tablecloth, because from the looks of things, he didn't have a patch of clothing on.

Ondine's pulse hammered freshly in her ears. *I'm going to have a heart attack before I make sixteen.*

'I'm nawt dead,' Shambles said at last.

Despite her concern for some modicum of decorum, a smile broadened her face and happiness bubbled in her veins. Heavens above, her dream had been wrong. Way wrong.

Those devilish green eyes stayed fixed on hers, while a lopsided grin added a mischievous gleam. Suddenly she averted her gaze and dropped her lashes so she could study the ground.

'I'm nawt dead,' Shambles said again, louder this time as he turned his hands back and forth in the moonlight. Then he wrapped the tablecloth around his middle, stood up and shook his head in amazement. He took a step closer and cupped Ondine's cheek in his palm. Heat seared her face. 'The dream didn't come true.'

'The . . . the . . .' *The dream? He knows about it?*

'You're not dead by a long shot,' Old Aunt Col said from the doorway, making Ondine and Shambles-Hamish turn quickly to see they had company.

'But if you lay a finger on my grand-niece, you'll wish you were.'

Indeed, they had an audience, including Ondine's mother who, from the shocked look on her face, had seen quite a bit too.

Chapter Ten

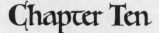

It was Ma who came to her senses first, ordering Shambles-we-should-call-him-Hamish-now to go inside and get dressed. She gave him some of Josef's old clothes[43] so he could dress properly. Tablecloths are only fashionable for attending a toga party, and this was not such an occasion.

'I look like a waiter,' he said, as he came back to the beer garden.

At the sound of his voice, Ondine turned and looked to the ground because she'd become used to

---

43 *They'd 'shrunk' in the wash during Colette's first pregnancy with Marguerite. Men often gain weight when their wives or partners are pregnant. Some call it sympathetic eating, others claim it's Couvade's Syndrome, where a man experiences the same pregnancy symptoms as his partner because he's so 'in touch' with her feelings. The most likely explanation is too many pies.*

Shambles approaching from a low vector and racing up her leg. But of course he wasn't a ferret any more, he was a real man.

Old black leather shoes, scuffed and somewhat curled up at the toes, came into view, then an expanse of black socks capped by the hems of his pants. Something made her stall over the hem, because she didn't want to look up any further, knowing what a furious blusher she could be.

'Sure, the pants are too short, but they're better than the tablecloth,' he said, taking a step closer to Ondine. 'Ye can look up, lass, ye won't turn to stone. Yer ma says she's made me look nice.'

If she'd known the word 'smitten', Ondine would have used it to describe herself when she looked into Hamish's face. Those green eyes glistened in the moonlight, making them seem dangerous, while his shock of black hair lay flat on his head, smoothed down into submission with gel. Ondine's palms itched to mess it all up again, as her face burned with fresh embarrassment.

What a man! If she'd thought Lord Vincent was

attractive, Hamish was off the scale.

To her deep, cringe-inducing embarrassment, nothing came out of Ondine's mouth, because she found herself thinking, *You look gorgeous*. But she didn't know if she'd actually said it out loud or not.

At that point, Cybelle walked past and made kissing noises as she headed back to the kitchen, shattering Ondine's illusion that they were the only two people on the planet. Everyone else in the garden looked at the two of them as well: Mrs Howser, Old Col, Melody, Ma and Marguerite.

Then Ma spoke up, 'It's all hands on deck tonight, people will be arriving for dinner soon. Hamish, head to the kitchen and help Chef and Josef, they're run off their feet. Ondi, it's not your engagement party, it's Margi's. Roll your sleeves up and get to the sink.'

Just like her mother to double-book the night. She probably figured with all the extra guests, she could rope some of them into waiting tables.

'Yes, ma'am,' Hamish said, and gave Ondine a look she couldn't read – although she felt something flip over in her belly – before he turned and left.

Of course they wouldn't get a moment alone, Ondine privately fumed as she followed him to the kitchen and pulled on an apron and an enormous pair of gloves. Sure, they were standing near each other, but at the rate the dishes piled up, there wasn't a chance to say any more than, 'Pass me another tea towel, this one's soaked.' And even though they had obviously been psychically linked in the dream she'd had, it didn't seem to work when they were awake. A few times she tried to psychically ask him to pass a towel, but he didn't.

Can you hear my thoughts? Ondine silently asked.

Hamish made no reaction, so she took that as a 'no'. She felt frustrated at her lack of psychic progress, but at the same time a little bit glad he couldn't read her mind right now.

Da kept looking askance at them, and shook his head a few times. Ondine could have sworn he chuckled too. Every now and then, Ondine caught her parents quickly discussing things in hushed tones, then they'd throw a glance her way. Probably just to make her feel paranoid.

Chef barely had time to acknowledge the new member of staff, because he was busy cooking a dozen steaks five different ways from rare to well done.[44]

Then another thought struck Ondine: with the new year of school starting at the end of summer, she would be away all day and writing assignments all night. They'd have to keep Hamish on to help out while she was busy studying. Surely her parents wouldn't put her education at risk?

Perfect logic.

The thought sent a glimmer of excitement through her system as she plunged her hands into the scalding water to scrub one of Chef's particularly nasty stockpots.

'Right you two, stop mooning at each other,' Ma said as she approached. They'd been washing dirty

---

44 *If you're the kind of person who likes steak 'well done', consider this.*
Do you like it incinerated because you really do want to get cancer from
eating burnt food, or is it because you can't handle the sight of blood?
If it's because you can't handle a bit of pink, then you're a wuss. Steak
should be well pink inside, and dripping beautiful bloody juices on to the
plate. And another thing. If you order your steak 'well done' you'll get the
lousy piece of meat, because the chef knows you don't know anything
about how real food should taste.

dishes for nearly an hour by this stage. 'You're both on front of house for the rest of the night, so do your best. Whoever gets the most tips earns a day off tomorrow.'

The thought of a day off – sleeping in, reading her favourite book, lounging about in her pyjamas until noon – held serious appeal. That and not being up to her armpits in greasy water.

Ondine turned to Hamish and pulled her hand from the glove with a noisy squelch. 'May the best one win.'

'You're on,' he said, giving her hand a friendly shake.

She should have been confident, but when his hand took Ondine's, her bones turned to mush and the intensity of his gaze made her forget what they were supposed to be doing. Then another thought occurred to her: perhaps she should throw the competition and make sure Hamish won?

'Stop making eyes, go clean up and get out the front. Dinner won't serve itself,' Ma said.

Ondine ducked out of the kitchen for a moment and returned wearing fresh, clean, *dry* clothes. It hadn't taken her long, but she was already running behind.

According to Ma, Hamish was out there charming everyone.

She took the plates of food to a family with four children and sighed. With a large family, there wouldn't be much money left over for tips. On the other hand, it would help Hamish get ahead in the race, so that wouldn't be such a bad thing.

Her competitive spirit kicked in when she saw the group of ladies at her next table. One look at their pastel blue hair told her they were retirees, most likely widows, possibly with a bit of cash to splash. She took their orders and they all said yes to dessert, plus tea and coffee. Turning back to the kitchen, she caught sight of Hamish as he farewelled an earlier group – all well-dressed and aged around thirty. They should have plenty of spare change. The resigned look on his face indicated otherwise.

'What's wrong?'

'Teachers. Lousy tippers,' he said.

'Why don't you take my table that just came in? Charm their socks off.'

Hamish cast a glance at the new group of women.

From the look of their showy earrings and manicured hands, they had plenty of cash to spare. 'You'd do that for me?'

'Sure, what are friends for?'

Hamish grinned, then stalled for a second as he gazed into Ondine's eyes. 'You're letting me win?'

A wicked smile split Ondine's face. 'No, I'm giving you an even chance. You'll make them feel young and pretty again; I'll just remind them of their long-lost youth.' Then she pretended to blow on her nails and shine them on her shirt.

Game on. Gimme your best shot.

Great Pluto's ghost, I'm reduced to thinking in clichés.

Picture the following: two old glass jars that once held industrial amounts of artichoke hearts and pimento-stuffed olives (which were very tasty, thank you) sitting on a shelf. As Hamish accepted the tips from one table, he dropped the coins and the occasional note into his jar on the right with a satisfying tinkety-clunk.

As Ondine accepted tips from her tables, she returned to the kitchen and placed half her tips in her jar on the left (again, with a satisfying tinkety-clunk) and the other half in Hamish's jar on the right. A person with nothing more to do than watch the tips jars all night would see the coins and notes clunketing and tinketing left and right, a few more for Hamish, then a few more for Ondine, who gave yet more to Hamish.

Anyone would think she was trying to throw the game.

In this case, absolutely true.

'Ondine, what are you doing?' Ma asked, arms crossed tightly over her ample bosom.

A large invisible rock formed in Ondine's throat as she tried to swallow. When she opened her mouth, nothing came out.

Hamish walked towards them with a spring in his step, his hands full of money, his voice a sing-song. 'Mrs G, here's the receipt and money from table ten for you, and the tips for me.'

Ma had to uncross her arms to take the money, but as soon as she took the notes she re-folded them. Holding her mother's eye contact proved too much like confrontation, so Ondine turned to check on Hamish.

On his face she saw the smile of a man with no troubles.

'Righto, let's count them, shall we?' He lifted a jar with each hand.

Time moved slowly as Ondine found herself unable to move her feet. Ma had her in some kind of suspension glare that kept her fixed to the spot.[45] The complete opposite of what she should do, which was to get out of there and join the rest of the engagement party in the rear garden.

Hamish seemed oblivious to all of it as he hefted the jars to the table. 'Let's see who's the winner.'

Ondine felt sure she saw a gleam in his eye. Sure enough, the gleam became a full-blown twinkly glisten

---

45 *It's a known fact that parents do have these super-powers, but only in limited supply. Many possess glares that can root you to the spot. Mum's spit on a hanky is the most powerful grime solvent in the known universe. They also have unlimited resources to make you feel guilty for doing just about anything even remotely out of line. They are also good at getting lids off jars with seemingly little effort, and know just about everything about anything, so you will never win an argument. Children of the world rejoice, for kryptonite is at hand. Make them breakfast in bed and tell them you love them, often. For then they will be yours and they will do your bidding.*

as he emptied both jars at once on to the table. The entire contents mushed and tinkled together in one messy coin pile.

Ondine's mouth fell open. He'd done it deliberately! Didn't he want to win?

'Oh dear, I guess I should have given that more thought.' He gave a nonchalant shrug.

A giggle escaped Ondine's open mouth. Despite her best efforts, she couldn't make it stop.

Ma uncrossed her arms, but only so she could put her hands on her hips. 'You two. You're incorrigible!'

Ondine snorted.

Ma conceded defeat. 'Fine, fine, call it a draw. Enjoy your morning off tomorrow.'

Hamish grinned and sent Ondine a look that made things dart around inside her in an altogether quite lovely way. Then his face fell. 'Morning off? I thought the winner got the day off?'

'Yes, but it's a draw, so a day off for one person becomes a morning off for two. Now, Margi's lot are still out the back, go join them.'

Typical Ma, Ondine thought, *always one step ahead.*

* * *

As they walked out to the back garden, Ondine stayed a few paces behind Hamish.[46] Soon she found herself under the full attention of her great-aunt.

'He must be mending his ways,' Old Col volunteered as she took a seat under a tree to settle in for the night. 'Although from the way he looked at you, Ondi, I can't vouch for how long it will last. Praise the heavens for a full moon, for there's nowhere to hide when Luna is watching us.'

'How come he's not a ferret any more?' Ondine asked the question she'd been dying to know the answer to ever since Shambles changed into Hamish.

Her great-aunt gave a theatrical sigh and shook her head. 'He must have found the motivation to break the spell. Let me think. What did I curse him with . . .'

As if you could forget something like that.

'Clearly, he wants to be human again. What do you think is happening?'

---

46 *It would be rude to suggest that she was doing that deliberately so she could get a look at his trim backside which fitted rather too snugly in Josef's old pants. But yeah, she looked, and it was good.*

173

'I have no idea.'

'Surely you do. He's bonding with you, I'm sure of it. Which leads me to wonder, what powers do *you* have that you can reverse one of *my* spells?' Great Aunt Col fixed Ondine with a beady eye.

Lurch went something inside her belly.

Margi spotted them and came over. 'Ondine, what happened to the fairy lights?' She pointed to the bundles of globes bunched up in a tree.

'Oh, sorry about that, I'll fix it,' Ondine said, grateful for something to do other than be subjected to Old Col's inquisition. Bless Margi, she'd rescued Ondine just in time.

But when she made to climb up the stepladder, she wobbled and nearly fell off.

Help was at hand. Melody came to her aid and held the ladder steady. 'Ondi, he's gorgeous,' she whispered.

The bundle of fairy lights tangled in her hands. 'Um, if you say so.'

'Are you blind? He's absolutely *divine*,' Melody said, fanning her face with her hand, pretending she'd become flustered.

'Cut it out!' Ondine hissed, desperately trying to stem the shaking in her hands and failing.

'He really likes you, too. I can tell by the way he looks at you. Do you think your mother will let him stay with you?'

'Oh, Melody, let it drop!' Ondine became even more anxious, but from the mischievous look in Melody's eyes, there was no way her friend would comply. As much as she loved thinking about Hamish, the thought of everyone else thinking about her and Hamish only added to her frustration. Her only chance of reprieve was to change the subject entirely. 'So, Mrs Howser, yeah?'

It worked. Melody looked confused and crinkled her forehead. 'What about her?'

'She and Old Col obviously go way back – they were less than pleased to see each other today.' Ondine felt giddily pleased with herself for so successfully moving the topic on to something much safer.

'Oh yeah, way back. They were good friends, but I found out from Mrs Howser that they had a huge falling-out at a debutante ball of all places. By the way, are you thinking of doing your deb? My mother wants me to, but they're *sooo* last century. All those dance lessons just for one night of dressing up. I guess that's what they did before television.'

'Mrs Howser told you that?' Now it was Ondine's turn to press for answers and watch Melody squirm.

'Not in so many words. I, um, sort of found out during an, uh, astral exercise.'

That was seriously impressive. 'Astral, eh? You're really doing well in that. And Mrs Howser has no idea you know all this?'

The conversation should have ended in them giggling, but what Melody said next made Ondine wish she'd never gone down this path.

'I think it was over Hamish. They each wanted the same man to partner them at the deb, but Old Col won out. But . . . I guess Col lost in the end, because Hamish got drunk and it all ended badly. You wouldn't think to look at them now, but those witches were both really pretty when they were our age.'

'Talk about carrying a grudge. Just for a stupid dance,' Ondine said.

'But if it was over Hamish, and he looked like that,' Melody fanned her face with her hand again, 'I can understand it!'

Ondine rolled her eyes. 'Promise me we won't have a falling-out over something as silly as a dance?'

'Of course not. And we won't have a falling-out over Hamish either, because he's so taken with you nobody else could get a look-in.'

Ondine's hands trembled with nerves and she dropped the bundle of lights on the ground.

Chapter Eleven

Despite the late hour, Marguerite and Thomas's engagement party kept going strong. In between duties in the kitchen, Colette and Josef made regular appearances in the garden and were on their best behaviour around Thomas's folks.

All night Ondine fought hard to keep her focus on the party when the whole time her thoughts strayed to Hamish in human form. If only he'd stayed back in the kitchen, it would have been bearable, but he had to keep walking around with trays of food, making nice with everyone. Like this for instance:

'Can I tempt you?' he asked a group of Margi's friends, offering a tray of canapés.

The dirty flirt! The girls all smiled and giggled and took the morsels of food. As soon as his back was turned they huddled their heads together and tittered with suppressed laughter. The same thing happened to the next group he approached.

Frustrated, Ondine deliberately looked away from Hamish and saw Mrs Howser sitting at a table, with a mixed group of Thomas's friends. What could they have in common? Then she saw it: Mrs Howser upended a teacup on to her saucer and turned it back.

Inching closer, she heard the old lady's predictions.

'. . . a carriage. You are going on a journey.'

Pfft, isn't everyone on a journey?

Ondine restrained her scorn but couldn't help rolling her eyes. Something she seriously had to stop doing, because it was starting to hurt the sockets.

'Read mine,' a girl enthused.

'You'll need to drink the tea first. Infuse it with your aura.'

'But I don't like tea.'

Stifling a snort, Ondine made to leave, but her mother, who just happened to be passing at that moment, had other ideas. 'Ask Ondi for your future –

she'll read it in your palm.'

A trickle of fear entered Ondine's soul. Expectant eyes turned to her. She felt trapped. She mouthed 'no' to her mother in protest, but the woman ignored her.

Is this Gang Up On Ondine Day?

'But, Ma, I'm not –'

'You should have seen her the other day! She had the health inspector nailed, right down to how many children. We passed the inspection with flying colours, by the way.'

'Read mine then.' The same young woman who didn't like tea sprinted towards Ondine with her palm out. 'Tell me what I'm in for.'

'She has the gift, it's in her blood,' Ma gushed.

Ondine didn't know what matricide[47] meant, but she was having thoughts of it all the same.

The window of opportunity to protest closed with a thud in her ears. The eager teenager held her palm out for inspection. The face that greeted Ondine looked so happy, so expectant. It would really

---

47 Unpleasant business. The result of which seriously dented Charles Lamb's writing career. Shakespeare suffered no such problems.

sour the party mood if she refused.

Promising to growl at her mother later, she set to work making stuff up.

'I'll need both hands. One palm is what you were born with, the other is what you make of it.'

She sensed Mrs Howser's eyes on her as she looked over the two palms. Scant weeks earlier, she'd fled Psychic Summercamp. Unfortunately it had followed her home. Time stretched. Nothing came into her head to help her out. Her own palms began to sweat. Her customer's palms were just soft mounds of flesh with lines on them. Pale, with a few blotches of red near the juncture of her fingers.

Eczema?

'You really need to watch out for allergies,' Ondine blurted.

'Ohmigosh you're right! I get terrible hayfever. What else?'

When Ondine looked up at the girl's face, she saw her smile, and noticed the very pale gums around her teeth.

'You're a vegetarian.'

'Wow. You're good!'

No, she wasn't good, just observant. Pink gums were an indication of good health. Pale gums showed iron deficiency, which meant the girl probably didn't eat meat. Observation and pure good luck. Hardly a sign from the heavens.

The guesswork should have put her customer off, but all it did was attract more people eager for the same 'divine' instructions.

'You have a kind heart and like looking after people,' Ondine said. Nobody in their right mind would disagree with that.

The girl withdrew her hands. 'I nearly forgot,' she said. 'I need to cross your palm with silver, don't I? Otherwise it's bad luck.' She drew a few coins from her purse and gave them to Ondine.

Money.

So that's why her mother was so keen to foster the psychic connection. They could make money from it! The realisation made her feel sick to her boots. It was one thing to engage in some harmless entertainment as a party trick, but when money was involved, it became outright fraud.

'No, please, this is just for fun. Keep your money.'

'Hardly. Last thing I want is a gypsy curse hanging over me. If you don't want the money, put it towards Margi's wedding. Now, tell me how I meet my husband, and how many children we'll have.'

'I'm next,' Ondine heard to her left.

'Then me,' another said.

'Start a queue then,' she heard her mother say.

Lurch went her stomach. *Fizz* went her brain.

She was done for.

Aside from her palm-reading swindle, the rest of the party was excellent. Less than half a dozen beer glasses broken, nobody came to blows, people laughed a lot, the police only came around twice to check on the noise and Margi and Thomas danced whenever the music played. The best part of the night – as far as Ondine was concerned – was Mrs Howser and Aunt Col retiring earlier than everyone else, both claiming 'a headache'. They'd probably sneaked back into the front bar to continue bickering. Or raid the plütz supply more like.

On the minus side, Hamish had spent the rest of the night walking among everyone. Correction, *flirting* among everyone, tempting people with plates of food. Whenever Ondine saw him, she had to fight the growing hunger pains in her tummy against the prospect of having her family see her talking with Hamish and making a fuss. It was best to keep clear of him completely and go hungry.

Da made a speech that started maudlin and got worse, lamenting about losing his oldest daughter, his first baby who would always be his baby. Funny, that – he'd told Ondine she'd always be his baby, that day at the train station. Surely by now he had to accept his three 'babies' were allowed to grow up?

'It's difficult for me, with three daughters,' he continued, looking at everyone through beer goggles.[48] 'When I was Thomas's age, I could never understand why the girls I liked had such strict fathers. Now I

_____

48 *Beer goggles make everyone look much more attractive than they really are. Especially at closing time when there aren't many singles left in the bar.*

understand. It's because every young man out there is just like I used to be!'

People howled with laughter and thumped Thomas on the back.

'But seriously,' Da continued, 'Thomas, you're a real surprise package. You're one of the good ones, and I'm pleased as plütz to welcome you to the family.'

To Ondine's complete surprise, the two men embraced in a manly hug. Her father was softening. Hooray for Margi!

Da's speech was tame compared to those made by Thomas's friends, which started in the gutter and ended up in the sewer. Margi blushed scarlet and Thomas yelled out, 'Who invited you?'

'You did!' they yelled back.

'I don't know these people!' Thomas buried his head in his hands.

Poor Margi, she winced and cringed so much during the ribald speeches Ondine felt sorry for her. Although just for a moment it was a relief to have someone else become the centre of embarrassment. When the speeches were over, it was time for more dancing, so

Ondine and Melody joined in with a large group of Margi and Thomas's friends. During one of the old-style progressive dances, Ondine twirled around the group and caught sight of Hamish standing in the doorway, watching her.

Of course, she had to trip right at that moment. Stupid shoes. When she looked up, Hamish was gone, thank goodness. She could get on with ignoring him properly.

'I see him looking at you,' Marguerite said as she sidled up to Ondine. 'Reminds me of the way Thomas used to look at me. He's working up the courage to ask you out.'

'I doubt it.' *I hope so.*

'Count on it.' Margi gave her a warm hug, then cast her eyes back to her fiancé. 'Would you look at that. Da and Thomas are into the plütz like old friends.'

'Who would have thought it?' Ondine said. 'Da's really coming round to the idea of Thomas joining the family.'

'You can thank Ma for that, she brought him round.

And Thomas too – he's been the *perfect* gentleman.'

Of course her sister would say that, being so madly in love with Thomas. Ondine tried to smile and be happy for her sister – truly she was – but sadness seeped in.

'Oh, Ondi, cheer up.' Margi noticed right away, of course. 'It may not seem so now, but one day you will be as happy as me. I know it.'

When the last of the guests left at around five the next morning, Ondine hobbled to a bench under the fairy lights and rubbed her aching feet. It felt good to soothe the knots and aches. As she massaged the sore skin, she felt as if someone were watching her.

'Yer family puts on a fine ceilidh.'[49] Hamish approached with a plate of hors d'oeuvres.[50]

Ondine tucked her feet underneath her skirts to hide how ugly her toes looked from being squished and

---

49 *A popular form of entertainment, with dancing and music, pronounced 'kay-lee'. Not to be confused with 'Kylie', which is another popular form of entertainment.*

50 *Fancy French finger food. Pronounced 'or-dervs' with a hint of garlic breath.*

mashed all night. She made to speak but her mouth went dry.

'Ye havenae eaten all night. If I didn't know any better, I'd say ye've been avoiding me, lass.'

'Don't be silly,' she said, surprised that she managed three words when her throat felt so parched.

'Here, eat.' Hamish grabbed Ondine's hand, making her hold the plate of food. At his touch, heat shot up her arm and she stared at the food, her appetite nowhere to be found.

'I like being human again,' Hamish said, tilting his head down so he could make eye contact with her lowered gaze.

A lock of dark hair fell over his forehead. An ache started in Ondine's heart. Heavens above, he was so handsome a girl could completely lose her head. As if to deny her feelings, she picked up a slice of savoury tart and shoved it into her mouth. It didn't matter that only moments ago she'd been touching her feet and her hands were probably covered in germs. All she wanted to do was stuff her mouth with food so that she didn't say something stupid.

Ordinarily she loved Chef's food. No wonder
Cybelle had fallen for him – the man cooked like an
angel! Yet right now, Ondine couldn't taste anything
because the presence of this Scot had invaded all her
senses and turned the food to dust.

'I need to tell ye something, Ondi.' Hamish's hand
touched the back of hers. Ondine's heart started
racing in her chest and the skin on her arm puckered
into goosebumps. 'Yer cold.' He took his jacket off and
placed it around Ondine's shoulders. 'There, fits ye
better than me anyway.'

A nod was all Ondine could manage.

'Ye don't like me any more?'

Ondine gulped down the hard lump of food as her
throat constricted. 'No, that's not true,' she replied,
but she didn't say anything else because her brain had
stopped working properly. She didn't say, 'Hamish,
I like you too much,' or 'Hamish, you're the most
handsome man I've ever met,' or 'Hamish, you'd
better ask me to marry you or I'm going to die right
now.' Although her thoughts took her exactly along
those lines.

'I'm no psychic, so I can't read yer mind. But I'll tell ye what's on mine,' he started.

Ondine forgot how to breathe.

'I've taken Old Col's advice to heart. I need to mend my ways. Tonight has shown me that. I have it in me, I can reclaim my life, and make it a good life too.'

Hamish shifted on the bench, and angled himself towards her. 'Ondi, can ye please look at me. I want to know ye don't hate me.'

It took an almost superhuman effort, but somehow she managed to get her head to turn enough, and her eyelids to lift enough, so she could look him in the face. Not his twinkling eyes, which would hurt her heart too much if she looked deeply into them. She settled for his lips. That was a mistake, because the moment she looked at his mouth she wanted to kiss it.

Stupid hormones. Turning me into an idiot.

'You've shown me that it's noble to be useful. To be part of a family. I've never had that before . . .'

What he said didn't make sense, because she barely heard half of it over her hammering heart. Was he saying he wanted to stay with her family, or was he about to return to his in Scotland?

'I've asked yer ma and da if it's all right if I can stay here. Just until I find me feet, like.'

Yippee! Hamish is staying. Hamish is staying. Hamish is staying. Oh dear, did I just say that out loud?

'I've relied on other people's charity for too long. I need to find my own way.'

Hey? Had she missed a segue? One moment he was talking about staying, then he talked about leaving. *Make up your mind!*

Then he seriously overstepped the mark and took Ondine's hands completely in his. 'Do me a favour and keep away from Lord Vincent.'

Fury took hold and her breath hitched. She pulled her hands away and felt her palms grow itchy. Oh, how she wanted to slap his smug face! It was bad enough that he was so beautiful, that he said such lovely things before ruining it all.

'You sound just like Da.'

'I want you to be happy, and I don't think Lord Vincent would make you happy.'

'So I'm not even allowed to have some fun?' she blurted out.

Hamish looked into her eyes and a lopsided grin changed his face from serious to gleeful. 'Aye, a girl like you should have some fun.'

The reprieve gave Ondine a chance to collect herself. Anyone else would have patronised her, treated her like a child, but not Hamish. Guilt stabbed at her heart. She owed him the same courtesy.

'Hamish?' She hesitated, not knowing what to say next. It was right that he couldn't stay indefinitely. Her parents were pretty generous, coping with everything that had transpired, but generosity has its limits.

He leant closer, his eyes focused on her lips. Closer. Closer, his lips descended towards hers. His eyes closed, hers followed suit, her heart hammering with anticipation and belly turning flip-flops as she waited for his lips to touch hers.

To her utter dismay, his lips touched her cheek instead.

'Jupiter's moons!' she exclaimed. If this was to be their first kiss (hopefully of many), she wanted it to be a good one. Seizing her chance, she held Hamish's face in her hands and pressed her lips directly to his.

An arrow-fast jolt of lust shot through Ondine and her breath hitched in her throat. His lips felt so warm and inviting, the pressure not much more than chaste but the contact made her whole body buzz and fizz. Time locked around the two of them, extending the moment, filling her heart with a strange mixture of elation and pride. She'd kissed him, really kissed him, and hadn't botched it up.

Hamish pulled back, his shining eyes locked with hers. The smile he gave her sent warm flurries all around her.

'Ye shouldnae done that,' he said, sounding like he, too, was short of breath.

'Why not?'

'Because now I have tae do this,' he said, parting his lips and pressing them back on Ondine's, coaxing her to open to him. She nearly lost her mind at the intimate contact and the swathe of sweet and strange sensations roaring through her body. The kiss deepened and she heard a soft moan escape from Hamish. Tiny electric shocks danced over her lips, his chin felt prickly against her plump skin. Beard whiskers grazed her.

'Ouch.' She pulled back and rubbed her fingertips over her inflamed skin.

A half-embarrassed grin spread over her face. Her first pash-rash? Expecting to see the same delight in his expression, she met his eyes just as they were turning from green to black.

Matching black fur spread over his face.

'Oh no, not now!' A heavy weight grabbed at her heart.

'What?' Hamish managed before he doubled over in pain, clutching at his belly. He reached to Ondine for support, and the skin over the back of his hand turned black and furry.

The sun rose for the new day, casting the beer garden into pink-orange light. The full moon was gone. A pile of second-hand clothes sat lifeless on the ground. Where Hamish the man had been, now sat Shambles the ferret.

Chapter Twelve

Swearing. Some people are good at it, some people trip over their tongues. Take the not-yet-sixteen Ondine, for example. Her swearing wasn't very advanced, because she'd had a reasonably protected life so far – as protected as a person can be while living in a pub.

For example, when she becomes frustrated or shocked, she will just as likely say 'Jupiter's moons!' as 'Clutterbuck!' (or something sounding very much like that). On the other hand, Shambles, who up until now had managed not to swear too much in front of the de Groot family, proved himself proficient in profanity.

'Ye chanty wrassler, A'll dun't ye!'[51] His accent came back thick and strong. 'A'll gar ye claw whaur it's no

---

51 *You liar, I'm going to bash you.*

yeukie!⁵² A'll saut yer brose,⁵³ Old Col! Ma tongue isna unner yer belt!'⁵⁴

He laid the brogue on thick. Despite the accent, some of the swearing required no translation, which only made Ondine's face burn with shame. Those lips she'd just kissed were spewing forth the most fearsome curses.

'Shambles, please calm down!' Her heart ached for the man he'd been not a moment ago. How horribly unfair that he should revert like this. Could the timing be any worse?

Despite her pleas, Shambles would not be stopped. He swore some more, with a few new expressions. After he'd exhausted his repertoire, he went back to the start and repeated the tirade all over again.

It was too cruel, watching him writhe about on the ground, her handsome young man reduced to ferret form again. Ondine felt her heart constrict, tied up like

---

52 *I'll put my fist where it's not welcome.*
53 *I'll get my revenge.*
54 *And don't even think about trying to silence me.*

one of Chef's string roasts. Heat seared her face and eyes. Something wet splashed on her cheeks. Oh for shame, she was crying! What was the point of trying to behave – and be treated – like an adult, if she ended up blubbering like a child who'd just found out Santa wasn't real.[55]

'What's all the racket?' Ma said, as she came out to the garden and took in the scene of Ondine crying with a black ferret at her feet. 'What did he do to you?'

'It's yer mad auntie, she's struck me down again, and I didnae do anything!' Shambles complained, rubbing his furry paws over his head in anguish.

'We only kissed,' Ondine said, surprised to hear her words come out as a croak.

'That's highly inappropriate, Ondine de Groot,' Ma said.

It's a sure sign of trouble when parents use your full name,[56] and Ondine knew better than to argue

---

55 *Sorry to break it to you. Santa's just a modern-day symbol of the Christmas season and the spirit of giving. Or rampant consumerism. Ach, dry yer eyes.*

56 *How to judge parental mood by the name they call you. e.g. Ondi = Ma in a good mood. Ondine = Ma is busy. Ondine de Groot = Ma is*

with her parents when they were in a foul mood. Actually, arguing with them at any point often proved a waste of time because she seldom emerged the winner. But all good sense had flown because their Beautiful Kiss[57] had ended too soon, as had Hamish's human form.

'It was just a kiss,' she found herself repeating in a tone that implied it didn't really matter, when in reality it *really, really* did matter. It mattered a whole lot. She'd become good friends with Shambles the ferret, but Hamish the young man seemed the answer to her dreams. How long had she imagined what he'd be like as a real person? Then to get a glimpse of his true self, to let him into her heart – only to have it taken away so soon. Could life become any crueller?

Shambles was still busy swearing. Loudly and lustily.

---

really narked. *Ondine Benedicte Wilhelmina de Groot = Ma's just walked in and Ondine's standing over a dead body with a bloody knife in her hand.*

57 *This had been her first Serious Kiss, so it required capitalisation. Considering Ondine was fifteen, it shows how protected her life had been up until that point.*

'Get inside, Ondine. I'd like to speak to Hamish alone,' Ma said.

'You're so unfair.' Ondine wiped the tears off her face with the back of her hand. 'I'm not a baby, so stop treating me like one!'

'We'll stop treating you like one when you stop behaving like one,' Ma shot back.

In frustration, Ondine's hands balled into fists. This was an argument she couldn't win, but she'd try anyway. 'You were my age when you and Da got together, so that makes you a hypocrite as well!'

'It was different then –' Ma started.

'Oh, blow it out your ear!'

Things went very silent. Ondine slapped her hand over her mouth in shock. She'd never spoken to her mother like that before, and the power of it made her heart hammer against her ribs.

Ma stood there, mouth agape. Even Shambles stopped swearing and moaning on the ground.

With lips pressed into two straight lines of fury, Ma straightened her shoulders and drew herself up to her full height, which was a couple of centimetres short of her youngest child. When had her mother shrunk so? Ondine wondered about this for a nanosecond before they resumed the mother–daughter showdown.

Her voice low and dangerous, Ma said, 'Show some respect for your elders.'

'Is that the best you can come up with? Speaking to me like I'm a child? Ma, I'm nearly sixteen. I'm allowed to kiss whoever I like!'

'It wasnae her fault,' Shambles piped up. 'It was all me doing. I took advantage of her, and that must be why I'm a ferret again. I had lusty thoughts and didnae feel worthy of her.'

Confusion knotted Ondine's brain. Their encounter had been nothing like Shambles described. The way she remembered it, Hamish had given her a chaste kiss on the cheek, and she'd demanded more. Her cheeks flushed with heat.

'It's "whomever".[58] Now get inside, Ondine – you're overtired.'

It must have been pure aggravation that made

---

[58] *What is it with parents always correcting your grammar? They'd never do it to their friends.*

Ondine say what she said next, because no rational person would have blurted it out.

'Oh yeah, fine, send me to my room. But while you've been so busy spying on me, you haven't even noticed that Cybelle and Chef are making eyes at each other.'

'She's just saying things. Don't listen to her,' Shambles said, but his intervention made no impact.

The colour drained from Ma's face and for the first time in Ondine's memory, her mother was at a loss for words.

A huge and theatrical yawn escaped Shambles's little mouth, as if he'd given up on both of them. Or he just wanted to clear the area for the oncoming catfight. 'I did me best, ye wouldnae listen. I'm for the laundry. Goodnight, ladies.'

Heavy, nasty guilt sank into Ondine's feet. She couldn't move. She'd just dropped her sister right in it, and Cybelle had done nothing to deserve it. If Ondine believed she was entitled to happiness, weren't her sisters entitled to the same?

Which made her a hypocrite of the highest order.

Between clenched teeth, her mother said, 'Go. To. Your. Room.'

Something made Ondine's feet move, although her brain felt so fogged she had no idea how she managed to find the way to her bedroom and crawl under the covers.

Sunlight pierced daggers through the curtain gaps. She feared sleep because of the frightening dreams that might come her way. Should she stay awake and feel miserable, or fall asleep and have her subconscious make her feel worse?

In the end, the choice was not hers to make. Despite the beams of early morning light in her room, Ondine passed into unconsciousness, just before the worst few hours of her life unfolded.

Chapter Thirteen

Ondine had the strangest sensation of having had a particularly awful dream. Shambles had become a real man, and a stunningly handsome one at that, but then some force took it all away and he was back to being a ferret. As her brain clicked and whirred into wakefulness, she knew it was no dream. Waking up further, she sprang out of bed and clutched her stomach. She wanted to be sick, and for so many reasons. Last night, she'd made a fool of herself in front of Hamish and in front of her mother. Topping it off, she'd robbed her middle sister of any privacy she might have enjoyed while her parents were distracted with Margi and Thomas.

There was a choice to be made. Get out of bed and face her mother and sister or stay in her room forever.

A staccato rap on the door put paid to any notion that it was hers to make.

'Ondi, get up, family meeting,' Da said.

'I want at her first,' Cybelle said.

With an angry look that could strip paint, Cybelle burst into her room and slammed the door behind her. Black panda smudges circled her eyes where the neat eyeliner used to be.

Nasty, heavy things tumbled around in Ondine's stomach.

'How dare you!' Cybelle's face was red with fury. 'Do you have any idea what you've done? Chef's going to get the sack because of you!'

'I'm . . . I'm sorry,' Ondine blurted. Hot tears sprang into her eyes and blurred her vision. 'I'm so sorry, Cybelle. I didn't mean it. I was so angry with Ma . . . it . . . it . . . just came out.'

Cybelle stood there with her hands on her hips, her lips pressed white in a hard, straight line. Just as her mother's had been the night before.

'Sorry's not good enough! You've just ruined my life. I hope you're happy!'

With that, Cybelle slapped her hard on the cheek. Pain seared Ondine's face, but she didn't put up a fight.

'I deserved that.' Hot tears splashed her face. 'Belle, I'm so sorry, I really a–'

Cybelle slapped her other cheek, spreading the pain. Behind Cybelle, Da charged in, grabbing his middle daughter in a bear hug.

'That's enough!'

Cybelle flailed her arms, kicked her legs out and screamed so hard bits of spit flew out of her mouth, 'I hate her, I hate her! She's not my sister!'

'Calm down, love. It's all right, I'll not sack Chef.'

Fresh tears sprang from Ondine, and she covered her face in shame. Heavy guilt roiled in her stomach and curdled her brain. All she wanted to do was stay in her room and cry. Her father would have none of it, demanding her attendance downstairs.

Not caring what she looked like, Ondine shrugged on a dressing gown and trudged down to the gathering.

Old Col sat regally at the top of the table, while Shambles stood before her, pleading his case, 'What did ye do to me, Col? I thought ye lifted the spell.'

'I did,' the elderly woman said with a tired shrug. 'I'm as much in the dark about this as you. My only guess is the full moon must have played some part. We all know there's nowhere to hide on the night of a full moon.'

'Spare yer epithets,' Shambles said, and he turned to see Ondine, Da and Cybelle walk in.

Da's mouth fell open in surprise. 'Ondi, I can hear him talk now.'

If her father could hear Shambles, it would save time with translations. It also eroded any last vestiges of privacy she might have had with him. Not that she deserved any privacy after what she'd blurted out about Cybelle last night.

Shambles nodded to Ondine to acknowledge her entrance, then resumed his pleading to Old Col, throwing his short arms around as he talked.

'But I didn't do anything wrong. We all *know* that. I was being responsible for the first time in my life. It was *just a kiss*, it was never going to go any further. Why would that make me turn back into . . . into this?'

Just a kiss had been the same words Ondine had

used. They were a lie so she could save face. But hearing Hamish-as-Shambles say it to someone else, with everyone listening, well, that was a different matter entirely. Maybe to him it was *just a kiss*, but to her it was everything.

Old Col looked at the ferret. 'Ah, but you see, Hamish, maybe this isn't a punishment after all. Maybe the full moon shone a light on the kind of man you could be.' Her eyes glistened with confidence.

Ondine had no idea what the old woman was banging on about. Forget sage advice, this was more like scratching around for answers like a chicken in a compost heap.

'Enough of that,' Da said, taking his seat at the other end of the table and pulling Ondine down beside him. Cybelle sat across from them so she could shoot her sister filthy looks. The fact that Cybelle also sat beside Chef was not lost on anyone, particularly Josef.

Incredibly, Ma stayed quiet as Shambles approached Ondine and climbed on to the crook of her arm. If this had been last night, if he'd been a man again, his touch would have sent searing heat into her bloodstream.

But it was the morning. He was a ferret again. What a passion killer!

'I am sorry about last night. I'm sorry I made ye cry,' Shambles said.

'It's not your fault,' Ondine managed, giving him a wan smile that didn't reach her eyes. Maybe he was a ferret again because she didn't want him to leave. Wasn't that what she'd been turning over in her head yesterday? If he became human again, he'd probably leave. If he remained a ferret, he'd stay with her.

The head of the household cleared his throat and directed his comments to Chef. 'I have a blinding headache from last night, so excuse my lack of manners. Henrik, I want to know what your intentions are with Cybelle.'

They could all tell by Da's clipped tone that it was not a request. And he'd called Chef by his real name for the first time in ages. Ondine's heart sank. Their father had been softening so nicely lately – now he seemed to have reverted to caveman mentality.

Cybelle kept her head bowed, her hands clenched into fists on the table. Every now and then she lifted her eyes to shoot Ondine a greasy look of utter contempt, before resuming her sulk.

Nobody said anything for a few seconds as everyone else's eyes fell on Henrik.

When Henrik spoke, his voice was quiet but determined. 'No, Josef. It's private. This is something between me and Cybelle, no one else.'

In shock, Cybelle lifted her head and smiled as she looked with pride at her paramour. Henrik glanced back at Cybelle, and traced his fingers over her white knuckles.

Nothing came out of Da for a moment, such was his surprise. He swallowed and started again. Like a spluttering lawn mower, it took a while before he got a good spin going. 'You *will* tell me, because it concerns my daughter, and your tenure here as an employee,' he demanded.

So he *was* about to sack him? Ondine couldn't believe how nasty her father sounded.

'Remind me never to play poker with your da,' Shambles whispered.

'I heard that,' Josef said, turning his now-famous

frosty stare towards Ondine, which nailed her to the spot. After he'd turned her blood to ice, he looked over everyone at the table. 'Who else heard him? Show of hands.'

Gradually, everybody raised a hand to about shoulder height, even Henrik.

'All of you?' Ondine blurted.

They nodded. Her heart sank. There really was no privacy in a large family and, judging by the extra people sitting around the table, hers was about to get larger.

Shambles piped up, 'That's great news! If ye can all hear me, it must mean the spell is breaking.'

Da turned to Henrik, waiting for an answer from his earlier question.

Henrik kept his voice low and steady as his eyes locked with Josef's. 'Mr de Groot, if you sack me, you'll be minus a chef. I'll go and find another job. But it won't stop me seeing Cybelle. Only Cybelle can decide that.'

A strange icy feeling spread through the room.

'That's right,' Cybelle said in little more than a

whisper as she touched Henrik's arm for support. 'If Henrik goes, I'll go too. Then you'll be short one chef *and* one daughter.'

Blotches of red bloomed on Da's face, while the veins on his neck doubled in size and threatened to burst. Ondine felt she might be sick from all the excitement.

'What he means is, he wants what's best for Belle,' Ma interrupted. 'We want you to be happy, sweetheart.'

'My head is killing me,' Da said by way of explanation. 'I know this is coming out wrong, but this is all a big shock to me.'

Henrik spoke again, 'It's only an hour till lunch, so if you want to sack me, better do it now, otherwise I've got work to do.' At that he rose from his seat.

Josef said nothing more. Henrik kissed the top of Cybelle's head, not gloating in victory, just confirming that he and Cybelle were united. A team.

A stab of jealousy pierced Ondine's heart as she watched her mother wrap her arms around Da's shoulders in comfort, while Margi rested her head on

Thomas's shoulder. Hope sank like a stone as she sat there with a talking ferret instead of the real man he should be, a real man she could fall in love with.

Things then took a turn for the worse as Ma looked towards her.

'Ondine, you may give me that apology now.'

It would have been so convenient if Melody or even Mrs Howser had come in at that point, to break the tension. No luck – they were sleeping off the party. As they weren't family, they'd been spared the meeting. A hard lump formed in Ondine's throat as she swallowed. She'd never shouted at her mother like she had last night, and it called for a grovelling apology. Everyone was looking at her, and it made it that much harder to deliver when all she wanted to do was crawl into a cave. Preferably one with a big rock she could shove over the entrance. Life as a hermit held tremendous appeal.

'I'm sorry, Ma.' Ondine's voice was barely above a whisper as she bowed her head.

'Didn't quite catch that,' Ma shot back.

Ondine tried to swallow again. 'I'm sorry, Ma.' This

time it came out like a squeak, but it was louder and at least her mother would hear it.

'For what?'

Ondine lifted her head and looked directly in her mother's eyes. 'I'm sorry, Ma, for being rude to you last night, and for answering back, and for implying you talk out of your ear.' Tears blurred her vision.

Ma smiled and said, 'Thank you, I appreciate that. Now you may apologise to Cybelle.'

Oh great, she had to go through it all over again.

'I'm so deeply sorry, Belle, for betraying your trust and telling Ma about something I shouldn't have.'

'I don't accept it. You had no right to say anything, you –'

'Belle, that's enough,' Da interrupted.

An uncomfortable silence descended around the table.

Ma cleared her throat. 'Good. Now go to your room, Ondine. You're grounded until I say so. I'll let you say goodbye to Melody and Mrs Howser, but that's it. And then we'll talk about changing your electives for school. Joining the ski team is no longer an option.'

Something heavy drained out of Ondine. It could have been her fighting spirit, or perhaps her sense of justice. Had her parents just taken her choices away from her? For what? Gossiping about her sister? She couldn't move her legs. Shock rooted her to the spot.

'You're going to take my ski lessons from me because I was rude?'

Da spoke up. 'No, we'll need to change your electives because we can't afford them any more.[59] You'll need to choose classes that have the least number of excursions and the cheapest text books. We now have two weddings to plan and they cost more than your education.'

'What?' Cybelle looked shocked. 'Why should I get married? I'm not getting married! Nobody gets married any more.'

---

59 *Brugel's government school system is nominally free, a legacy from the Soviet days. However, parents are required to make 'voluntary' payments in exchange for copies of their children's term reports. There are also fees for subjects that incur extra costs for excursions or equipment. The most expensive electives are winter sports (ski fees) and media studies (camcorder fees). Both these subjects were high on Ondine's list of electives.*

'I don't care how modern you think you are, there are some traditions I insist on. You are getting married. That is one argument you will not win,' Ma said.

Forget her sister not wanting to get married, Ondine was still reeling about her curtailed studies. 'But what about all the jewellery and money you kept?'

It was Ma's turn to blush. 'It's gone, Ondi. We spent it on renovations. That's why we couldn't afford to close the dining room last night. We need everything we can get.'

Shame and frustration made Ondine's chin wobble out of control. To add to her misery, she felt hot splashes of unrestrained tears on her cheeks.

Just kill me now, my life is over.

'And leave Shambles here. He's not to be in your room again.'

'I'm sorry, lass,' Shambles said, leaning up to give her a cold, wet and a little bit whiskery kiss on her neck.

There was nothing for Ondine to do but trudge up to her room and rot.

Chapter Fourteen

A couple of hours after the horrible and soul-destroying family meeting, somebody tapped lightly at Ondine's bedroom door.

'What?' she moaned, not even bothering to disguise the misery in her voice.

'It's only me,' Melody whispered. 'Can I come in?'

'I'm grounded. I'm not allowed to have friends anymore.'

Melody came in anyway, and closed the door behind her with a soft click. 'I heard about what happened. It's awful.'

As she stepped closer, Ondine noticed the girl had a floppy, leather-bound notebook in her hand.

'You'll have to narrow it down. It's *all* awful,' Ondine said, wiping her nose on her sleeve. 'Hamish turned back into a ferret, Cybelle hates me, I'm grounded, and my parents can't afford to pay for the classes I want to do because they want Belle and Chef to get married. Be careful Ma doesn't find you in here – she'll ground you too.'

'She can't ground me,' Melody said.

'Nah, you're right, she'll just ground me twice.' Ondine sighed. Pitifully, with all the pathos she could muster, she said, 'I know why they call it grounding because it grinds you into the dust and makes you give up hope.'

'Then I came just in time. Look what I found.' Melody held out the book for Ondine to see.

It looked soft and old on the outside, and inside the pages had handwritten notes, except for the ones at the back that were left blank.

'It's someone's diary. But it's hard to read because the writing's all scrunched up,' Ondine said.

The diary pages had a freshness about them, as if it had been sealed up in the dark somewhere for a long time.

'I think it's Old Col's,' Melody offered, her eyes

opening wide with wonder.

'Where did you find it?' Ondine tried to make out the scrawled handwriting. Squinting didn't work. She held the pages further away from her face. That didn't work either. 'It's all just scrawl, page after page of it.'

They looked at the pages in silence, trying to make sense of the bunched-up lettering. 'Where did you find it, Mel?' Ondine asked again.

'Um . . . Look at this page, I think I can make out what it says.'

Avoiding the question confirmed Ondine's suspicion. 'Did you steal it?'

'Oh no, I would never steal,' Melody said, making a crossing movement over her right breast.

'The heart's on the left side.'

Hastily, Melody made a crossing motion over her left breast before confessing, 'It came to me in a dream.'

Ondine's jaw fell open in shock. 'You went into Old Col's dreams? How did you do that without her knowing?'

For a moment Melody found something interesting

to look at on the bedspread. 'I'm getting pretty good at it,' she admitted.

'Not good enough,' a strong voice said from the doorway.

They both looked up to see Old Col standing there.

'You really must be more careful with your dream-catching, young lady,' Old Col said, walking in. 'Honestly, it was all I could do not to burst into a fit of giggles. I haven't seen anyone that cack-handed since . . . well, Howser never was any good at it, and now she's passing on her mistakes to you. Come on, make room on that bed for an old lady, I need to rest my bones.'

Too shocked to question their instructions, the girls moved apart and made room for Old Col between them. The woman took her sweet time lowering her frame to the bed.

'If you knew Mel was in your dream, why didn't you hide the diary?' Ondine asked.

'Because this way was much more fun,' her great-aunt said, and added a wicked laugh. 'For a girl who's grounded, you sure got a lot of company. Shambles, you can get out from under the bed now.'

Confused and stunned, Ondine picked her feet up and folded them under herself, then peered over the edge of the bed to see Shambles slink out from underneath. 'When did you get in there?'

'Sorry, Ondi. I was going to say something . . . but . . . well . . . it would have been rude to interrupt,' he said. For a ferret, he looked a bit sheepish.

'Right, Mel, pay attention,' Old Col said. 'This is my diary, and I let you find it, because I am old and I get my fun when I can. Naturally, you can't read it because I wrote it in code. Shambles, Ondi, this concerns you both because I've got the spell I used on Hamish in here somewhere. Right, let's find the page I'm after . . .' She licked a wrinkled finger and stabbed at the page corners to turn them over. 'Getting close now, hmm, no, can't read that out, that's private, OK, next page, no, that's private as well.'

This went on for some time, and Ondine couldn't help fidgeting and wondering whether anyone else would walk past and notice all the people in her room. She darted a quick look at Melody and saw that she, too, was fidgeting.

'Now it gets interesting, I've just met a handsome young laird called Hamish McPhee, and he's utterly charming.' Old Col lifted her eyes from the diary and glanced at the ferret. 'That would be you then.'

A weird feeling overcame Ondine. She wanted to know everything that had happened between Hamish and Old Col at that fateful debutante ball, but at the same time she wasn't sure she really wanted to know. Or at least, she knew she wanted to know, but it felt awkward knowing that Old Col would know that she knew. And Melody too.

'Found it. I thought Hamish wanted to court me, but he's not interested, just like all the oth– . . . um, let's see what else I've written.'

Ondine could have sworn her great-aunt was blushing. What had she nearly said? It sounded suspiciously like 'all the others', which meant exactly what?

Maybe she hadn't been an old prude her whole life. Then another, scarier thought pinged across her brain. If she turned Hamish into a ferret for messing up her debutante ball, what else was she capable of?

'What others?' Hamish stood up to his full height

(which wasn't very tall) and put his hands on the equivalent of where his hips should be if he were a man. 'How much others have you turned into like me?'[60]

A tingling sensation stole over Ondine's skin and she silently thanked Hamish for asking the question she dared not utter. This could get very juicy. They just had to stay quiet and let it unfold. Now, if she could just find a way to let Melody know about shutting up, they could –

'You mean there are others like Hamish?' Melody blurted out.

Too late!

'Do you want to hear the curse or not?' Old Col said, her voice sounding testy as she scanned through the pages. 'Because I can very well take the diary and go.'

'Please stay, Aunt Col,' Ondine begged. 'We need to hear the curse so we can figure out how to reverse it permanently.'

'You girls remind me so much of how we used to

---

60 *In times of great stress, people's grammar often flew straight outs the*
windows.

be, Birgit and I. We were good friends – we used to do everything together. I'm not sure how, but as we got older, we started to get pretty competitive. I had my gifts, she had hers. When Hamish came on the scene, our competitive streak turned to jealousy. We should have known Hamish had a mind of his own, but each of us thought we could control him. I . . . gosh, I can't believe I did this, but I cast a spell on him just to drag his sorry self to the debutante ball in the first place. He was such a handsome man. Quite turned my head. Ah dear, the things we do. It seemed so important then, but in hindsight, vanity got the better of me. Just once, I wanted to feel like a princess. Birgit was so much better looking than me, y'see. But *I* had Hamish on my arm for the ball.'

For a moment the old woman batted her eyes as if she might be crying, then she righted herself and kept going.

'Everybody was looking at me, and I felt wonderful. Birgit was furious and said she'd never speak to me again. But it didn't matter at the time because I had Hamish. Only, the enchantment started to wear off because alcohol and free will have a stronger pull than magic. I wasn't to know that at the time, having never touched the stuff until that point in my life.[61] If I'd just let Hamish have his say beforehand, he might have partnered me anyway. But you see, I was too jealous of Birgit. I wanted to make sure I had the best date. So I made him think he wanted to dance all night with me. Except he came to his senses soon enough and knew I'd tricked him.

'Not even the strongest magic in the world can make people do something they really don't want to do. Hey, Hamish?' Col looked at the ferret on the floor.

'Sorry, Col. I wes pretty young an' stupid meself at the time.'

Old Col wiped her eyes and flicked through the book. 'Right, the curse, let's see . . . oh, here it is . . .'

You revolting little weasel. How dare you break my heart?'

---

61 *While it's true Colette Romano did not drink alcohol until she was nearly twenty-five, she made up for it pretty quickly after that.*

'It's not one of my better ones.' Old Col absently scratched her face.

Melody looked confused. 'It doesn't even rhyme. I thought all spells had to rhyme.'

'That's just what Birgit Howser would have you think. Don't worry, it gets worse.' Old Col cleared her throat to read the next part of her curse.

**You can stay like that for all I care.
You're all the same, you lot.'**

'See, I completely destroyed the metre as well. Put that down to the heat of the moment, I guess,' she said with a shrug.

'That's it? That's the curse?' Melody asked.

'Told you it wasn't one of my better ones, although it's lasted longer than I thought it would,' Col said.

Ondine rubbed the patch of skin between her eyebrows to help her think. 'So, if he's been a ferret all this time, does that mean you don't care? Is that what it would take to get him back?'

Old Col closed the book. 'I'd best get out before

your ma finds me in here and I get grounded too.'

'I'm still in the room ye know, ladies. Can we get back to the issue of how I get back to me regular self?'

They all looked at Shambles. He cleared his throat. 'I hev a theory. For most of the years I've bin like this, nobody could hear me. But now people can. The curse is wearing off, so it is. I've reformed since Ondi took me in, truly I have. Surely that's enough to make ye care?'

'I do believe you have, Hamish,' Old Col said. 'I swear to you, I do care, and I have lifted the curse. You've had a glimpse of the man you once were, and can be again. The rest is up to you.'

At her great-aunt's words, Ondine couldn't help thinking about the glimpse she'd had of the man Hamish could be. And That Beautiful Kiss. It was the kind of sense-memory that stayed with you.

Shambles looked up at Ondine and their gazes locked.

Please be human again, Hamish.

Please kiss me again, Hamish.

Chapter Fifteen

As it transpired, Ondine's 'grounding' was not the usual kind. She was isolated in her room for most of the day, but her parents allowed her out for kitchen duty when they had customers. Considering they had customers nearly all day long in the bar and dining room, things didn't feel that much different from her normal life.

For the rest of the day, Shambles kept his distance, but she told herself that was because he didn't want to cause more problems or get her into trouble. To add to her punishment, hardly anyone talked to her, the dark looks Cybelle gave her notwithstanding.

They were incredibly busy that night. Ma set Ondine to work in the front dining room instead of scrubbing greasy dishes. There she stood, pencil and paper in hand, ready to walk into a room full of people, grinning to herself.

'I'll be fine.' She stepped out into the public arena and took the orders from table six. It was Mrs Howser's table, and she'd invited some friends to dine with her. They wanted the set menu. Too easy.

'I can do this,' Ondine said to herself as she headed back to the kitchen to give Chef the details. The beautiful smells of the busy kitchen invaded her senses, but she ignored her growling tummy as she gave her table's order to Chef.

Her voice cracked, making the word 'six' sound a lot ruder than it should have. 'Four sit meals for table sex,' she said.

Any moment now searing heat would pour up her neck and face.

Huh? Nothing. How strange.

For a man who had every right to be furious with Ondine, Chef Henrik looked pretty calm. 'Thanks.' He took the note and stuck it to the metal stove-hood with a magnet.

'Right.' *Keep going on with work and act as if*

everything is completely normal.

Down the other end of the kitchen, Melody stood with her sleeves rolled up, washing plates.[62] Ondine rolled her eyes. Her parents had even got her friend working!

Ooompfh. She turned and walked straight into Cybelle, whose arms were filled with dirty plates.

Arms filled no longer.

The load crashed to the floor with a clang of cutlery and a smash of breaking plates.

'I'm so sorry.' Ondine scraped up the mess with her hands and threw the pieces in the bin. 'I didn't see you.'

Through clenched teeth, Cybelle said, 'You did it deliberately.'

With her usual, uncanny sense of good timing, Ma appeared. Their mother knelt down with a dustpan

---

62 *Anyone whose parents run a restaurant will attest that these things do happen. Friends who come home with you after school think it's 'fun' to iron tablecloths and do the dishes. That is, until they realise at the end of the night the parental units think it's all 'fun' as well, and give lollies instead of cash payment for work done. Said 'friends' will then never come back.*

and brush to sweep up. 'Happens to the best of us. Ondi, get back out front of house and take table seven's order. Belle, everything's OK.'

Straightening herself out, Ondine stood at the kitchen door and drew a steadying breath before she faced the public. Just as she took her first step, she felt a hard push in her back and she sprawled forwards, arms whirling. For a horrible sickening moment she thought she'd land face-down on the carpet. At the last nanosecond her feet came forward. With a wobble she righted herself, and ran a nervous hand through her hair. The push in the back had to be Cybelle's doing, but having an argument in full view of the public would only prove that restaurant reviewer correct.

Pasting on a smile, even though she wished for the ground to swallow her whole (something she knew would never happen, but that didn't mean she stopped wishing it), Ondine headed to table seven.

'Did you enjoy your trip?' Lord Vincent asked. His face split with a smile.

Omistars he's here. He's here and Ma sent me out deliberately to his table when she could have sent Belle.

'Er, yeah, just tripped on the new carpet.'

Again she waited for the furious blushing. Again it didn't come. Did that mean she was getting better at handling boys? Confidence returning, Ondine stood poised with pencil and paper. 'Are you ready to place your orders?' she asked.

Lord Vincent gave her a devastatingly gorgeous smile that made her insides go flippy-floppy. To keep on the task at hand, she turned to the rest of the people in his group. She had to do something to stop naughty thoughts invading her senses. If Lord Vincent tried that inside-wrist-kiss again she'd melt into a puddle.

Only the night before, she'd seen the true Hamish and decided he was far more handsome – and attainable – than Lord Vincent. But that was because she never thought she'd see Vincent again. Now Vincent was here and Hamish was a ferret once more, and she couldn't help losing her head a little bit.

She mentally told herself off for being so inconsistent with her affections.

Lord Vincent said, 'Thank you Ondine,' after she took their orders – top-range stuff too, none of this we're-only-students-we'll-order-the-cheapest-thing-on-the-menu-and-then-share-a-dessert stinginess. With Vincent's smile fixed in her mind, Ondine's feet barely touched the floor on the way back to the kitchen, although she kept a keen eye out for Cybelle to avoid another collision.

'How is table seven?' Ma asked as she walked past, her arms full of plates of delicious, steaming food.

'Dreamy,' Ondine murmured, then gave a mental shake of her head as she heard her mother chuckle.

For the rest of the night, Ondine kept her distance from Cybelle and had only necessary conversation with Chef and the odd sly smile from her mother. Lord Vincent, on the other hand, seemed keen to talk every time she delivered food or took their plates away or refilled their carafe of water. His friends had excellent manners, Ondine noted – knife and fork placed together in the centre of the plate when they were finished, instead of a scrunched-up napkin.[63]

---

63 *Seriously, what's with the scrunched-up napkin in the middle of a dirty plate? It looks revolting. Have you any idea how hard it is to get blueberry roulade stains out of linen napkins? Just line your knife and fork together across the centre of the plate, with the tip of the knife*

'That was delicious,' Vincent said, locking eyes with Ondine and making her heart skip a beat.

Delicious indeed. 'I'll pass your compliments on to the chef.'

'Is the beer garden open tonight? We might take our coffee out there.' His gorgeous eyes burned into hers. The noise of the restaurant died away, making Ondine feel like the world only existed for the two of them. Her brain felt woozy and sluggish under his attentions, as if she'd been at the cooking sherry. All the while, her pulse beat loudly in her ears.

'Let me set up a table for you. Give me a couple of minutes and I'll come back and get you.'

'That sounds promising,' Lord Vincent said with a saucy grin.

This time Ondine did blush, as that familiar bothersome heat seared her skin, but she turned away before he could see how much he'd affected her.

Outside, they still had the fairy lights in the trees from Margi and Thomas's party, so she turned them

---

at twelve o'clock. If you've grown up with digital clocks, seek urgent deportment lessons.

on and set to work, flicking the tablecloth into the air and laying it down on to a table. The last time she'd done this, Shambles had raced in and skidded along the top, before turning into a very handsome man who'd delivered Ondine her first real kiss.

And he'd warned her about Vincent.

Jealousy did strange things to people, Ondine thought.

But she missed Hamish all the same. Yes, he was still around (judging by the copious sausages Chef kept turning over on the stove), but the rules of her grounding meant they shouldn't talk to each other.

But oh, how she missed him. Seriously missed him, which was more than she thought was good for her. What was the point of falling in love with a man if he turned back into a ferret when the moon went down?

Falling in love! Oh no, that's not what she meant to think at all. Not when she thought she might have the attentions of Lord Vincent. Admittedly, he was completely out of her reach socially, but a girl could dream, couldn't she? And he'd asked to be seated outside and was flirting so outrageously with her, he must be interested, surely?

Then why had her thoughts been filled with the delicious Hamish?

Gah! Ondine shook the images from her mind as she straightened out the wrinkles in the tablecloth, all the while chiding herself for such foolishness. If a person looked up 'confused' in the dictionary, it would say 'Ondine de Groot'.

'Beautiful,' Vincent said, strolling outside. There were no clouds tonight and the moon along with the bud lights cast small amounts of magic over the garden.

Ondine kept straightening out the tablecloth, even though it didn't need doing. Anything to keep busy. To keep from falling under Vincent's spell.

'It is a beautiful garden,' she managed. Something tugged at her, reminding her to keep thinking of Hamish.

'Not the garden, you.' He closed the distance between them.

How did a girl respond to that? A sensible girl would say, 'You're very kind. Now I'll bring out the tea and coffee orders for your table of friends,' but by this point 'sensible' and Ondine had long parted company.

She giggled.

Like a twit.

Burning heat spread from her neck all the way to her forehead. If only her feet would work, then she'd walk out of here and back into the kitchen. Even with her shove-in-the-back sister, the kitchen was a much safer prospect right now.

No such luck. Vincent took a step closer while Ondine stood mute. Another step, and he was only a metre away. Less now as he took another step.

One more step and they were almost touching. His hand cupped her chin. Tingling heat spread over her skin and down her body, making her pulse hitch in her throat and her mouth turn dry.

Quick, find something to say, or this is going to get way out of hand.

Her brain fled as Vincent's lips slowly closed the distance between them.

She tried to swallow, but her tongue stuck to the roof of her mouth. Her voice croaked as she blurted out, 'How come your da wants to close us down?'

Vincent paused a centimetre from his target.

'Don't talk about my father. I don't want to be thinking of him when I'm with you.' His voice sounded smooth and hypnotic.

When his lips came down on hers, Ondine expected to swoon, but she didn't. Instead her eyes flew open while his cold, wet tongue darted into her mouth in an altogether uncomfortable and completely baffling experience.

There was even a bit of slobber.

Ondine's hands came up and pressed against Vincent's chest, keeping their bodies apart, but only just.

'Stop fighting it, you know you want it.' His lips continued to make a mess of her face.

'This isn't going to happen,' Ondine said, surprised at how confident she sounded. A girl of her years should have been revelling in the intimacy, but instead it felt . . . not wrong, because that would mean she felt something. No, this was more of a sad hollowness, a disappointing sequel to their earlier encounter.

How quickly her emotions had changed. She

would have sworn she'd heard birds singing in her head when she'd first laid eyes on Lord Vincent. Now she felt a bit grubby as he continued his Braille conversation.

'That's enough.' Ondine pushed Vincent backwards, so that their faces were a good few centimetres apart and she could breathe properly without having him pressed so tightly against her.

'Now you're going shy on me? Take what you can get, honey, I won't offer again.'

Anger bubbled in Ondine's veins. 'And I won't accept either. I'm going back inside.'

She took a sideways step to get past him, but he blocked her exit, his nostrils flaring. 'No you don't. Not until I get what I came for.'

Cold, horrible, paralysing fear glued Ondine to the spot.

'L-leave me alone,' she said, only it came out as a squeak, so she said it again, hoping it would come out stronger. Nope, still a squeak.

'Where is it?' Vincent said, closing the distance again so they were almost nose to nose, body to body.

Each time Ondine took a breath, her breasts touched his chest.

No more squeaks. All she could do was whisper, 'Where's what?'

'Don't play dumb with me. Where's the money?'

'I d-don't know what you're —'

Slap! Lord Vincent's hand came down hard across her face. His voice took on a growling demand. 'Where's the money?'

Her cheek burned, but it didn't hurt as much as her heart, which felt like it could shatter into a million pieces. 'I'm going to scream,' Ondine whispered, but her squeaky voice made the threat completely pathetic. All the while her pulse hammered in her ears.

'You have one sister damaging the piano and the other's howling at the moon. *Nobody* will hear you. Now tell me where the money is.'

Trapped. Utterly trapped. In the quiet, between the thudding of her own heart, Ondine could hear loud music from inside the pub. Vincent was right; they wouldn't hear a thunderbolt out here, let alone one sad girl's screams.

Her face stung from his slap, but it was more a pain of disappointment. She thought she'd been a fairly decent judge of character until now.

'We've spent it,' Ondine confessed.

For a second Lord Vincent's face fell, before a nasty sneer took hold. 'Nice try. I almost believed you. Tell me where it is.'

'I've told you we sp–'

His hand flew up, ready to smack her again.

'It's inabox underthefloorboards inthepub,' Ondine blurted. With a burst of strength she didn't know she had, she pushed him away and made a run for it.

A hard hand gripped her arm, swinging her back so sharply her shoulder felt like it would pop out of the socket.

A growl came from deep within Ondine. 'Get your hands off me!'

The back door swung open and a murderous scream erupted. 'Arrrrgggghhh! Hands off what's nawt yers!'

Familiar black fur blurred past Ondine. Relief washed over her at Shambles's timely intervention.

'What the . . .' Vincent stumbled backwards in shock as something raced up the leg of his trousers. A howl of pain sprang from his throat as he fell down with a thud, hard on his bottom. Then he battered madly at his leg with his hands. 'Get off!'

'Leave her alone!' Shambles cried out.

'I am, I am.' Lord Vincent swatted at the rapidly moving lump under his trousers. He managed to hit himself a few times, which made him wince. Changing tactics, he stood up, crazily shaking his leg to free him of the demon possessing it.

With a battle cry of victory, Shambles rolled away from Vincent's leg. Then he rounded on his victim and gave him a nasty swipe against the ankle. It drew blood.

'Stitch that, Jimmy!'

'It talks!' Vincent gasped at the sight of his pint-sized enemy.

'I don't just talk, pal,' Hamish said, swiping at Vincent's ankle again and making another cut.

Vincent made to stomp on his attacker, but Shambles darted out of the way, then doubled back and charged up Vincent's leg.

'A ferret!' Vincent tried to shake him away before he could reach anything sensitive. 'You set a ferret on to me? Say goodbye to the hotel, I'm going to close this place down!'

With her heart beating a tattoo in her chest, Ondine felt her body trembling all over from fear and indignation.

'Yer all pish and wind,' Shambles said as he leapt free of Vincent and then made for the safety of Ondine. When he reached her shoulder, he made ready to launch himself at Vincent's stricken face.

'That's enough, Shambles. I think he's got the message.'

'You're finished, witch!' Vincent said. 'I'll have you charged with treason.'

'Oh really?' Shambles asked. 'Exactly how'r ye gonna explain what ye were doin' when ye got cut, eh?'

The colour drained from Lord Vincent's face. The shock value was priceless.

Courage stirred in Ondine. 'Everyone knows Shambles is always with me, and I'm happy to tell people what you tried to do to me. So go ahead, tell everyone you came off second-best to a ferret.'

They stared at each other for a moment, but it was Vincent who blinked first. 'Watch your back,' he said and made to leave. The words carried a veiled threat, but his voice cracked in the middle, exposing it as nothing but bluff.

'I'd watch yours if I were you, and your legs,' Ondine said as Vincent walked out of the side gate of the garden. 'We'll send the dinner bill to yer da.'

Shambles yelled out, 'And ye'll need ten rabies shots, all of them in the a–'

Ondine slapped her hand over Shambles's mouth. 'No need to be rude.'

'Ah, yer a feisty one! I'm real proud of ye.' Shambles gave Ondine a wet, whiskery kiss on the cheek.

Proud of her? Well, that was about the best thing she'd heard all night. 'Thanks, Hamish. I'm glad you arrived when you did.'

What a mess she'd made of things! Why, when she had someone as beautiful and funny as Hamish to look forward to, did she even contemplate an idiot like Lord Vincent?

Because he may never be Hamish again!

'Did he hurt ye, lass?'

There were so many different levels of hurt a person could feel. 'I guess not, but . . . oh, Hamish, you tried to warn me about him, but I wouldn't listen. Go on, say "I told you so".'

'Nay, lass, you don't need to be told anything. You're far smarter than me.'

'You're just saying that.' Ondine brushed off the comment as she made to return to the kitchen. She was still grounded; any prolonged absences would make her mother suspicious.

'No, I'm *nawt* just saying that. It's true. And thanks for calling me Hamish, it's nice to be treated like a person again.'

Something made Ondine stop at the back step. Here she was, growing older by the day, feeling frustrated because everyone treated her like a kid. All the while the adult male on her shoulder fared little better because of his present ferrety incarnation.

'If it helps any, you're a real person to me. And I hope the spell wears off permanently soon so you can be yourself again.'

Please be you again, Hamish.

Shambles gave a wickedly deep chuckle as they walked down the hall. 'Sure, yer just saying that, lass, cos ye want another kiss. I wouldn't mind another meself. Yer very good at it.'

No heat of embarrassment this time, but a wide grin split her face at the thought.

Shambles chuckled, then stopped suddenly. 'What are we doing in the laundry?'

'I'm pretty sure this is your room and, as I'm grounded, I'm not allowed to have anyone in mine. That includes you.'

'Nobody will notice. And you can't expect me to stay down here, it's all reekie.'[64]

For a moment Ondine stood still, wondering what to do, but then Shambles made her mind up for her.

---

64 *'All reekie' means 'smelly'. Not to be confused with Auld Reekie, otherwise known as Edinburgh.*

'Ye were giving it laldy[65] on that eejit, but yer still in shock and I think someone should keep an eye on ye, and as I was there, it may as well be me.'

'Why am I regretting this already? You're sleeping on the end of the bed, OK? *Above* the covers.'

'I wouldnae have it any other way.'

As they approached the kitchen, Shambles peeled off Ondine's shoulder and begged Chef for leftovers. Things were winding down for the night, with only a few tables left to receive their desserts.

'Lord Vincent had to leave,' Ondine told her mother. It wasn't exactly a lie. 'We're to send the bill to the Duke.'

Her mother's face took on an air of concern. 'What happened out there? You don't look so good.'

'And I don't feel so good either. Da was right, Vincent's a total pain in the . . . neck.' She wanted to say worse, but good manners turned up in the nick of time.

'You should go to bed,' Ma said, touching the

---

65 *'Laldy' means 'to do something with great vigour', whether delivering a beating, using a credit card or playing the piano.*

back of her hand to Ondine's forehead.

'Vincent knew about the jewellery, and the money. I don't know how, but he did.'

'Oh dear.'

'Exactly.'

'Right.' Ma was quiet for a while, as she thought what to do next. At the same time, she put the coffee on and set up cups and saucers. Not only could she talk about five things at once, she could practically do them as well. 'Things won't settle down out front for another hour at least, and you look ready to drop. Your father's retired early for once, Thomas is doing a great job at the bar. You get some sleep, then we'll talk about it in the morning.'

No second invitation needed. Ondine was only too glad to head to her room and collapse. Sometime during the night, Shambles arrived and made good on his promise to stay at the end of the bed.

'Settle, lass. I can't sleep with yer feet kicking me all the time.'

'Stop fidgeting then.'

A knock came on the door. 'Ondi, are you in there?'

'Quick, Hamish – under the bed, Ma's coming in,' Ondine whispered, then called out to the door in a louder voice, 'Where else would I be?'

Instantly she wished she'd kept her mouth shut. Already in enough trouble, answering back to her parents again could make things worse. Especially if Ma walked in and found she had company. Ondine couldn't think of a worse punishment than being stuck in her room whenever she wasn't needed for work, but her mother had no such lack of imagination and would be bound to come up with something more heinous. The furry black streak disappeared under the bed, his claws skittering on the floorboards as Ma opened the door. Thank goodness for creaky hinges drowning out the sound!

'Ondi, I'm sorry things went so badly with Vincent tonight. I thought your father was overreacting about him. Turns out his instincts were spot on,' Ma said, positioning her well-cushioned self on the end of the bed, right where Hamish had been. 'I told your da everything that happened –'

'But nothing happened!' Ondine protested.

'Sweetheart, it's not your fault, and you have nothing to feel embarrassed about. Vincent's the one with the problems, not you.'

'But . . . how did you know?'

'Hamish told me, because he was concerned for you.' Ma embraced Ondine in a hug and gently rubbed her back. 'We all think you've been very brave and Vincent's going to get what's coming. Aunt Col's looking into it. She could turn him into a toad or a slug. Which would you prefer?'

Ondine smiled in relief. And hey, Ma had called Shambles Hamish again.

'It's good to see you smile. I have some more good news. I was going to wait until the end of your grounding to let you know about school, but you need cheering up. Ondi, we do have the money. You can take the classes you want.'

Hope sparkled in Ondine's veins; she would have a life again! Then confusion made her head turn fuzzy. 'But . . . but why did you say we didn't?'

'Because I wanted you to think about your actions, and to realise that they have consequences,' Ma said.

After the altercation with Lord Vincent, Ondine hardly needed a reminder, but she was also intrigued by their sudden return to wealth. 'So . . . how much money do we have?'

Ma gave her a knowing smile, then kissed her on the forehead. 'Enough. Not enough to be silly with, but enough. It's getting late, you should go to sleep,' she said, closing the subject.

Part of Ondine wanted to give her mother a good old-fashioned yelling at for scaring her so much. Another part wanted to wrap her arms around her and hug her till they both dissolved into tears. The second idea won out.

Tears poured out. 'I love you, Ma.'

'I love you too, sweetheart. But better save your tears for the morning, Ondi. Aunt Col is leaving and she'll be taking Shambles with her, so they can work out a way to reverse the spell for good.'

Cold dread snaked around Ondine's heart and gave a squeeze. 'Tomorrow?' she croaked.

'I'm afraid so. Just as well he's back to being a ferret, otherwise I'd be worried you might try something stupid. And then I'd have three weddings to plan instead of two. I'd best be getting back to the kitchen. Goodnight, dear.' With that Ma closed the door behind her, leaving Ondine feeling confused and frustrated.

Old Col would be taking Hamish with her? Then another thought smacked her. Three weddings? Her parents were so stuck in the past!

The minute you're interested in a boy they want to marry you off.

From underneath the bed, she heard, 'Want to try something stupid?'

To her shock, she saw Hamish looking up at her. The real Hamish McPhee, not the ferret but the man. With a devilish grin on his face.

Chapter Sixteen

'You're . . . you're you again!' Ondine said, although she fought to keep her voice down in case she alerted anyone else to Hamish's sudden change in circumstances.

A roguish smile split his face. 'Aye, and I'm all skin no fur, so throw me a coat, will ye? And ye might want one for yerself, yer looken peely-wally.'[66]

Ondine leapt from the bed, half in shock, half in excitement. Her mind ran through several scenarios.

'You're human again, so that means you don't have to leave with Old Col tomorrow. You can make your own decisions. I mean, you can still go with her if you want, but you could just as easily stay. I'm

---

66 *Pale or blanched. Like when the colour drains from your face when a gorgeous man suddenly appears under your bed.*

sure Ma would appreciate the extra labour.'

'Draw breath, lass. Yer sounding just like yer mither, jumping from one thing to the next. Now give me a coat, I don't intend to spend the night under yer bed with fluff bunnies in me jacksie.'

Ondine trod softly to her wardrobe to fetch her biggest coat. The last thing she needed now was her mother back at the door, wondering who she was talking to.

Except her mother would say 'to whom she was talking'. Gah! Even in her thoughts she could hear the corrections.

'You look ridiculous,' Ondine whispered, as she covered a giggle with her hand. Her biggest coat barely fitted over Hamish's broad shoulders. Two long, hairy legs poking out underneath completed the silliness.

'We'll need to get yer da, borrow his clothes for a while until I can get some of me own.'

'At this time of night? I don't want to be the one to wake him. It's his first night off in ages. You've seen him grumpy. If you rouse him now it'll be like poking a wasps' nest. I'll find you a spare room for the night and we can see him in the morning.' At that, Ondine reached into her jacket pocket for her bunch of keys and found them missing. She checked the other pocket as a rising sense of panic made her hands tremble.

'I can't find my keys! I must have dropped them outside or left them in the kitchen or something.'

'Or that toerag took them.' Hamish practically spat the words out. He stripped the bed covers, grabbed the top sheet and wrapped it around himself like a bad kilt. In the process he gave Ondine a quick flash of firm upper thigh. Just how a girl was supposed to concentrate with such a distraction was beyond her.

'Think about it,' he said, tucking the fabric around his waist. 'Why else would he want to get ye alone?'

Why else indeed? Ondine thought with a sagging heart.

'I didnae mean to say it like that,' he added.

So he could read minds now? Ondine shook her head. The man was blunt, but he was also right. The whole thing with Lord Vincent smacked of a set-up, perhaps from the night she first laid eyes on him.

'The night we warned the Duke . . .' she started.

'Eh?' Hamish interrupted.

'Vincent was there in the palace – he was listening to us when we spoke to his father. And now he knows about the jewellery and the money. Maybe he knew all along?'

'Aye, nawt much gets past ye.'

Ondine slumped on to the side of her bed, and Hamish sat close beside her. Too close, making the hairs on her arms stand up.

'Be honest with me. You saw all of this coming, didn't you?' she asked.

For a moment he was quiet, then he turned to face her, taking her chin in his fingers. 'I didn't know at first, but I knew I didn't like him. He told his da his friends had been sick after eating here, and the Duke believed him, and that's when he set the health inspector on to us.'

A furrow crept over Ondine's brow. 'You told me to be careful, and I didn't listen.'

Hamish swallowed as his gaze bored into Ondine. 'There was a lot going on. We've all been pretty busy.'

'It's sweet of you to say that.' She wouldn't have listened to sense because she'd been so smitten with the handsome lord. Someone had paid her attention and she'd ignored the warning signs.

Ondine shook her head. 'And there I was thinking it was all because you were jealous.'

Hamish gave her another comforting smile. 'Aye, I *was* jealous. How could I compete with the son of a Duke?'

You were competing with the son of a Duke? For me? The thought cheered Ondine immensely until she directed her thoughts back to the problem at hand.

'And now that *son of a Duke* has stolen my keys. We'll have to get new locks in the morning. Da will be furious,' Ondine said.

'Unless he breaks in tonight.'

'Oh dear.' Ondine made for the door. 'Grumpy or not, I'd better get Da.'

'No, wait. I have a better idea.' A warm hand landed on Ondine's shoulder, sending more whirly things through her system. 'If Lord Vincent's planning on making a return tonight, let's give him a welcome to remember.'

He gave her a grin hot enough to melt her slippers.

* * *

'All set?' Hamish asked.

'I think so,' Ondine said, trying – and failing – to stop her hands from shaking as she oh-so-carefully laid a single strand of fake pearls across the top of the jewellery box. 'You're sure this will work?'

'Nope, nawt at all. He may nawt even come tonight, and tomorrow we'll change the locks so after that we won't have to worry. But he'd be a fool if he didn't send someone over before he thinks you've noticed the keys are gone. Ach, this coat is too tight.'

When Ondine turned, she saw Hamish pulling the coat off with a fair amount of force, giving her a magnificent display of his lean chest and arms. If her hands were shaking before, they were full-on trembling now.

Thank goodness it was dark, he wouldn't see how much she was staring at him. The one saving grace in all this was the complete lack of searing heat up her neck. She'd finally stopped blushing. Although in the darkness he wouldn't have noticed. Stupid hormones. Why didn't they work properly in the light of day?

What was the point of not blushing if nobody was around to witness it?

The shard of moonlight exposed his marvellous bare chest only an arm's length away, sapping her concentration.

'I'll make some coffee, to help us stay awake,' she offered. Partly to help them out, but mostly so she could clear her head for a moment and get away from him, to catch her breath. Drinking the coffee was not an option – she felt jittery enough thank you very much.

Suddenly she heard a noise.

'Hawd yer wheesht.'[67] Hamish's strong hand grabbed her arm and pulled her down to the floor, where they hid behind an upturned table.

No translation needed for Ondine. She clamped her mouth shut and breathed as silently as she could manage, while the close contact with that male flesh made her pulse hammer in her ears. It made so much noise she was sure Hamish – or their intruder – could hear it.

In the many books that Ondine had read, she'd

<hr />

67 *Shut up, sit down, hold your tongue and pay attention.*

often come across descriptions of men. They could be brutal or whiny, fat or scrawny, nervous or domineering, have funny gaps between their teeth or nervous tics. But nothing had prepared her for the reality of being this close to . . . the real thing. The real flesh and blood, the very masculine scent of him invading her senses, how he could be so naughty and charming and then so confident all at once. A girl could easily lose her head. Just as Aunt Col must have.

And then he'd let Old Col down in a very public way, embarrassing her in front of her friends. How could one person be so much fun, but such a liability?

In silence, they heard a key turn in the lock. The front door made a soft shudder as it came away from the jamb. Footsteps padded on the new carpet. From their hidden position behind the table, they watched the legs move about. At first they walked over to the fireplace, checking inside it and among the ashes, then over to the piano, where they heard the lid lift up and close down with a soft 'tunk'. Ondine thought they'd put the jewellery box in a really obvious place, but it still took an agonisingly long time for the intruder to get anywhere near the goodies.

Come on, come on, Ondine prayed silently.

At that moment Hamish's warm hand pressed over hers in unspoken support, as if he'd heard her. She looked at his face. He held his index finger over his lips to indicate their need for absolute quiet. The pulse coursing through her system had other ideas as it banged away in her ears.

In the silence, something made a horrible – and loud – snap.

'AARRRRGGGHH!' the thief cried out. He pulled his hand from the jewel box and shook it all around, their pre-set rat trap clamped over his fingers.

Hamish pushed the table back and they came out of hiding. All the while the thief kept screaming in agony, in between torrents of swearing.

In a blur of movement, Hamish grabbed him by the collar, forced the man to the ground and sat on him.

'Ye right there?' Then he grabbed a bottle of blue food dye out of his pocket and squirted it over the man's head and down the neck of his shirt, staining his skin good and proper. Ondine grabbed the man's free hand (the one not turning red from the rat trap) and held it steady, so Hamish could douse that with more food dye.

Hamish cried out with victory, 'Haha! Caught red-handed, or blue-handed in this case.'

'Need a *hand?*' Ondine asked, as she turned the restaurant lights on to reveal the identity of their thief.

Ondine's father, with his stubbly face and messy, sticky-up hair, chose that moment to stagger into the restaurant. 'Oh dear heavens,' he blurted as he took in the scene.

It couldn't have looked good. In fact, it was any wonder the old man's heart didn't give out on the spot. His daughter wearing pyjamas, a man who used to be a ferret wearing nothing more than a bed sheet around his middle, and the son of a duke lying screaming on the floor, with a blue face and his hand caught up to the knuckles in a rat trap.

'We caught him in the act, Da, he was trying to break in and steal all that money we found. So me and Hamish set this trap and –'

'*Hamish and I,*' Josef corrected.

'He stole my keys earlier tonight, so *Hamish and I* were waiting for him. We thought he'd send a lackey but he was stupid enough to come himself.'

It would have been a heavy silence passing between them if not for the whimpering Vincent on the ground trying to budge the rat trap off his hand.

Josef looked down at him. 'I'm calling your father,' he said.

Several furtive looks passed between Ondine and Da, as well as Hamish and Da, and then back to Vincent.

'Get the old man in then, and let's get this over with,' Vincent said, blowing air on his swollen knuckles. They looked red and cracked. For a moment – but only a moment – Ondine felt sorry for him as she removed the metal trap from his joints. Would his hand recover?

'Sit tight, Hamish,' Da said as he turned to leave the room. 'I'll call the Duke.'

Dad has his number? Interesting.

When Ondine turned back to look at Vincent, she could have sworn she saw a smile playing over his face.

Strange that he should smile when the shock of the events might give his old man a heart attack.

'Mercury's wings!' All the pieces fell into place. 'You wanted to get caught so the trauma would give the Duke a heart attack. You can't wait for him to show up. You were there that night when we came to warn the Duke about the attack at the station. You were there at the station, and you knew what was coming because you organised the whole thing. How dare you! You ought to be ashamed of yourself.'

'Good luck trying to prove it,' Vincent said, sounding more confident than he had any right to, considering the circumstances.

'You're forgetting one thing. I'm a witch,' Ondine said, overcome with a fresh bout of shakes at how daring she sounded. 'I'm from a long line of witches and I can read your thoughts. You want your father dead so you can inherit. Right now you'd pretty much like me dead as well but that's beside the point.'

A snarl grew on Vincent's face. 'Nice try. As soon as my father turns up with his lawyers I'm out of here.'

'He's on his way,' Da said.

And now Ma, Old Col, Melody, Mrs Howser, Cybelle, Chef, Thomas and Marguerite all appeared in various stages of wakefulness. For the first time in Ondine's memory, Marguerite's hair looked messy.

Another thought raced through her head: *since when did Chef and Thomas start spending the night in the hotel?*

'Hamish!' Ma, Mrs Howser and Old Col said together.

'Evening, ladies,' Hamish said back, still sitting on the disgruntled Lord Vincent.

Everyone looked at Vincent and then back to Hamish, then they all started asking questions at once.

'What's going on?' Margi asked.

'What's he doing here?' Cybelle asked.

'When did Hamish come back?' Ma asked.

'Is that Ondine's bed sheet?' Old Col asked.

'Oh, he's gorgeous!' Melody said.

It took a while to explain everything. Ondine felt grateful when the Duke finally turned up.

Then things got ugly.

Chapter Seventeen

Who broke the silence first? Vincent, of course. 'Father, thank God you're here. They've kidnapped me and are holding me for ransom,' he said. 'They're all in on it – they planned the attack on you at the railway station too. Look what they've done to me! Charge them with treason.'

It took all of Hamish's strength to hold him down on the floor.

'That's complete rot. He stole my keys earlier tonight so he could break in and burgle us,' Ondine said in their defence.[68]

'Don't listen to them, they'd say anything,' Vincent countered. 'Ring the police!'

---

[68] *The fact that 'Brugel' is an anagram of 'burgle' is a total coincidence.*

Sickness threatened to overwhelm Ondine. Who would the Duke believe? Or should that be whom? *This is no time to worry about grammar.*

'Shut up, prat!' Da thundered, then he turned to the Duke and modulated his voice. 'I apologise for being the bearer of bad news once again, Your Grace. It is hard to believe your flesh and blood can be anything less than perfect. However, Vincent *was* attempting to steal our takings from tonight. From what I understand, he may well have been attempting to steal the virtue of my youngest daughter as well.'

Embarrassment pinged through Ondine. Now everyone would know.

For a moment the Duke looked at Vincent with concern on his face, and Ondine felt something twist in her gut.

'If I may make a suggestion,' Hamish said, still sitting on top of their would-be burglar. 'We're all in our pyjamas, and he's come dressed to steal.'

Brilliant! Ondine beamed a smile at Hamish. He beamed one right back at her, making her insides feel all funny. She should have felt embarrassed at the intensity of his smile, but Hamish had just saved their collective skins. She had every right to beam with pride at how clever and quick he'd been.

'And if we wanted to kidnap your son, we'd have stayed anonymous. So why would we call you here?' Ondine added.

Hamish beamed at her again and she liked it.

The Duke looked mightily annoyed as he glared at his wayward son. 'I warned you, you stupid boy. I've signed the papers for Fort Kluff.[69] You're shipping off tomorrow.'

Veins bubbling with happiness, Ondine grinned at Hamish while little things fluttered and flip-flopped inside her tummy.

'Ondine,' the Duke began, 'lately it seems, whenever there's trouble in my life, you're there to stop it. Your information saved my life at the station and now you've saved my family's reputation. I don't think we

---

69 Brugel's top military school. Technically it's a reform school with nicer uniforms. And guns. Which is pretty disturbing when you think about it — they take the worst delinquents from the richest families, then teach them how to use weapons.

could have survived the scandal if this had gone public. Thank you.'

She beamed with happiness and curtsied, then realised the unsaid 'between the lines' kind of implication. Everything that happened here tonight must be kept private.

The Duke continued. 'Mr and Mrs de Groot, I apologise for the grief I caused your family in sending the health inspector. That was Vincent's idea and I should have checked things out for myself before acting. Two of my best advisors have retired in the last year and I find myself lacking . . . information . . . from people I can trust.'

Then he looked at Ondine and a puzzled expression flashed across his face. 'How old are you, Ondine, really?'

'Your Grace, I'm fifteen.'

'Good. I appreciate your honesty. Now, where is that ferret I saw you with?'

Her eyebrows shot up into her hairline. He'd remembered that? Perhaps the hotel's new name had jogged his memory?

'Aye, that would be me,' Hamish said.

Now it was the Duke's turn to lose his eyebrows into his greying hair.

Squashed beneath Hamish, Vincent let out a groan of misery.

'I got yer son a good one earlier tonight,' Hamish said. 'On the leg.'

Time slowed down for a moment as the Duke digested the information. A pang of sympathy in Ondine felt completely appropriate. After all, a man wearing a bed sheet, with a foreign accent, had just claimed to be a ferret.

The Duke's mouth opened and closed a few times. Perhaps he needed to unlock his jaw so his ears could open more.

To add to the general confusion, some of the hotel's paying guests, wearing dressing gowns and sleeping caps, turned up to check out what was going on.

'Nothing to worry about,' said Da. 'We'll provide complimentary breakfast to compensate for your disturbed sleep.' He encouraged the rest of his children and soon-to-be in-laws back to their respective rooms, and told Melody and Mrs Howser, 'It's all under control.'

Out of the corner of her eye, Ondine saw her mother lingering in the kitchen, listening in on the conversation.

The Duke's eyes twitched as he looked over Hamish. 'You say you are the ferret? In that case, change into one.'

Gulp went Ondine. *What if he can't? It's all my fault. I spent so long wishing him to be a real man, maybe he won't be able to change back. Then the Duke will think we're liars. And if he thinks we lied about a man being a ferret, he'll start to think we've lied about everything else.*

Still sitting on Lord Vincent, Hamish adjusted his toga. 'I'll do what I can.'

A look of concentration crossed his face and his eyes rolled back under his eyelids.

It was a tense time for Ondine. As much as she loved seeing Hamish in his human form, if he couldn't become a ferret again on command, they'd be in a whole world of trouble.

Relief washed over her as Hamish groaned and

clutched at his stomach. He started to shrink and grow dark. His face – that handsome face – turned furry. It was painful to watch, but Hamish must have been in even more pain.

While everyone stood dumbfounded in wonder, Vincent bucked the suddenly reduced weight off his back and sprang up to make his escape.

'Hold it!' Flinging his arm out, Da leapt forward and clotheslined Vincent, sending him sprawling.

'*Khaaak!*' Vincent coughed. 'That's assault!'

'I didn't see anything.' The Duke didn't take his eyes off Hamish as he reverted to his Shambles form. You could tell by the way he stroked his goatee with his pinky and ring finger that he was thinking really, really hard about what he'd just seen.

Panting, Shambles looked up at the Duke, then across to Ondine. The tip of his nose looked pale and he swallowed a lot.

'Well, I'll be.' The Duke clapped his hands. 'I've seen some magic in my time, but that's mighty powerful. How do you do it?'

Shambles the ferret panted on the ground,

gathering his strength. 'It's a lawng story.'

The Duke turned to Ondine. 'You are too young to serve alcohol. You could not have been working in the bar that night. It wasn't you who overheard the plot against me, was it?'

Twist, lurch, flip went her belly. 'You are right, Your Grace, I wasn't in the bar. It was Hamish . . . I mean, Shambles. That's what we call him when he's a ferret. He was under a table and he overheard the whole thing. He was the one who encouraged us to warn you of the plot against your life.'

'I've never seen anything like it. What an incredibly *convenient* talent to have!' the Duke said, still shaking his head as he looked at the ferret on the ground.

Ondine didn't think it was very convenient at all.

'I wouldnae call it that,' Shambles said, clutching his stomach.

The Duke stood there. All the while a smile played over his face. 'You must tell me, Ondine, how does he do it?'

'It's a strong enchantment,' Ondine said. 'My great-aunt, Colette Romano, cursed him, and only recently he's been able to rediscover his human form.'

'Hmm, how very interesting,' the Duke said.

Ondine blushed furiously. Mercury's wings, what an inconvenient time to start blushing again. She managed a squeaky, 'Hamish is very glad to be human again.'

'You'd make a good politician.' The Duke winked at her. It had a strange effect in that it should have been friendly, but it creeped her out.

This doesn't feel right.

'Your great-aunt is the one with the magic?' the Duke asked. 'She sounds like she'd make a wonderful ally. Would she be here by any chance?'

Something prickled in Ondine's conscience. If the Duke had Old Col under his command, how far would he take things? Sure, the old woman had acted in frustration against Hamish, but that was a one-off. At least, Ondine *hoped* it was a one-off. But what if someone like the Duke ordered her to turn other people into animals? Would her great-aunt be able to refuse?

'Did somebody ask for me?' Old Col appeared at

the kitchen doorway, her eyes wide and innocent. Like she just *happened* to be nearby.

Listening in, more like.

'Your Grace, this is my great-aunt Colette.' Ondine made the introductions.

'May I congratulate you on your good work, madam,' the Duke said. He took her hand and kissed the back of it.

'Why thank you, Your Grace.'

The Duke's face looked younger, brighter. Like he was having a Very Good Idea. Great even. At that point, one of the Duke's drivers came in and whispered something in his ear. The Duke whispered something back. The driver nodded, then clamped his hand on Vincent's shoulder and marched him outside.

On the floor, Hamish was still a ferret. The Duke stared at him and shook his head again. 'I've seen so many things . . .' The man used to making speeches seemed temporarily lost for words. Turning to Old Col, he said, 'I have need for talent in my employ, and you have that. What else can you do apart from turning men into ferrets?'

Old Col did a slow blink, then said, 'I can keep secrets.'

'An excellent quality.'

Metal screeched inside Ondine's head. *Did the Duke of Brugel just offer Old Col a job? What kind of job would it be?*

On the floor, Shambles began changing back into Hamish. Much to Ondine's relief. Seriously much. It looked painful, though, as if someone were punching him in the belly. From the inside.

It caused another look of wonder to cross the Duke's face. 'Bravo!' He clapped. 'That's very, very good. When I came here tonight I thought I would be in for a bad night indeed. Shambles and Ms Romano, you have cast a silver lining on events, wouldn't you agree?'

'Thank you, Your Grace,' Old Col said.

'Aye,' Hamish said.

The Duke played with his goatee again. 'Like I said, I have need of good talent, and you fit the bill. Hamish, you're brave and . . . *adaptable*. You're not afraid to tell me the truth and you think on your feet. I value that.

How would you like to work for me?'

Oh no, this is not good at all. Hamish is supposed to stay here with us, not go off and work for the Duke. Buzzing filled Ondine's ears as she waited for Hamish to politely refuse the offer. Surely he'd want to stay with them?

'In what capacity?' The voice belonged to Ma, who had been standing quietly behind them.

Thank goodness for Ma, she'll make it easier for Hamish to say no.

The Duke smiled and looked far too self-assured. The more confident the Duke looked, the more unsteady Ondine felt.

Pure confidence filled the Duke's being. Steady shoulders, non-twitching face, hands palm-outwards. 'Shambles, in your ferret form, you could provide me with invaluable information. You see, the Duchess lunches on a regular basis with her . . . friends. She needs a companion with a clear head and an eye for detail. Many people take advantage of our hospitality, whether at court here in Venzelemma or at the country estate in Bellreeve. It pains me to admit it, but valuables are going missing. I will be run off my feet when parliament resumes in autumn. Having someone looking out for me will prove most useful.'

It sounds like spying. Hamish would want nothing to do with that.

'Go on,' Hamish said, making a mockery of Ondine's thoughts.

'Nothing so hard as working here, I dare say, and you will be well compensated,' the Duke said.

But . . . but . . . Hamish wants to stay here.

'Sounds tempting,' Hamish said, putting Ondine's old coat back on. All the while Ondine's pulse roared in her ears because she wanted to stop and ask a dozen questions but felt too terrified to speak.

'You want him to spy on your guests?' Old Col crossed her arms over her chest.

Instead of denying it, the Duke laughed. 'You are right, my dear woman, that is exactly what I need you to do. In a nice way, of course. Ms Romano, Shambles, what do you say to joining my employ?'

Say no, say no, say no. Say you want to stay here. I don't like this. He calls you Shambles when you're Hamish.

'You'll pay me to make sure nothing gets nicked?

I say a big yes to that. I could do it with my eyes closed,' Hamish said.

Ondine looked at Hamish and back at the Duke. Why did Hamish accept so quickly? Didn't he realise if he went to work for the Duke, they'd hardly see each other? Maybe on weekends . . . but that was when the hotel was busiest and then Ondine wouldn't have any time to see him.

The more Ondine thought about it, the sadder she felt. Why, they'd hardly see each other at all!

What counter-offer could she have that would make him stay at the hotel? Judging by the silence from her parents behind her, they had nothing to suggest.

Old Col smiled (a bad sign) and said, 'Your Grace, I humbly accept.'

The Duke beamed with happiness. 'I am in your debt. You will begin the first week of September.'

Oh no. No, no, no, no, no!

Chapter Eighteen

The worst thing in the world had just happened right in front of her eyes, and nobody realised! If Hamish worked for the Duke, Ondine might never see him again! What a disaster! He'd be so busy, he might forget about her! He might even fall in love with someone else!

Ondine's head hurt from all the exclamation points!

After the Duke had gone, sleep proved impossible. Apart from the fact that she didn't have her bed sheet (Hamish had taken that for his toga), everything felt wrong. Tossing and turning held no appeal at all, so she made her way down to the kitchen for some warm milk. Maybe that would help?

She didn't see Melody until she nearly crashed into her.

'Can't sleep?' Melody asked.

'Got that right.' Ondine gave a dramatic sigh to prove her point, then set about raiding the fridge. 'You neither, huh?'

'Um . . . yeah.'

A troubling thought scudded[70] through Ondine. 'You weren't trying to read my dreams, were you?'

Melody looked at the ground, as if there were something very interesting in the tiles. 'I'm sorry, Ondi. It's just that I know something big happened here tonight with the Duke, but Mrs Howser pulled me away before I could find out. And I really want to know.'

No privacy during her waking hours, now Melody wanted in on her private thoughts. 'You don't need to read my dreams. Just . . . ask yourself, what's the worst that could have happened tonight? Because that's exactly what did happen.'

'Vincent got away?'

'Worse than that. The Duke offered Hamish a job.'

---

70 *'Scudded' is so a word. It means 'thoughts that shoot through'. Just like Scud missiles, sometimes they hit their target with devastating effect. More often than not, they go way off course.*

'But that's great!'

Frustration made Ondine slam the refrigerator door. 'No it's not, it's terrible!'

'It is?'

Ondine wanted to scream. 'Yes, it *is*. Hamish will be *ages* away and I'll never get to see him.'

'But . . . he'll still be *around*. I mean, it's not like he's going all the way to . . . I dunno, New Zealand or something.'

'New Zealand? Where's that?'

'Not sure, but I think it's really far away.'[71]

'Oh.' Ondine poured herself a mug of milk and put it in the microwave. 'It's just . . . I thought Hamish liked it here.'

'He likes *you*, that's for sure.'

A smile stole through, despite her pitiful mood. 'You think so?'

Melody laughed. 'Ondi, stop hunting for compliments. Hamish really does like you. And I know you like him.'

---

71 *New Zealand is about the furthest away from Brugel you can get on the planet. If you try and get any further away from Brugel, you'll start getting closer again.*

'So why is he leaving?' She nearly added the word 'me' at the end of the sentence, but reined it in just in time.

Melody shrugged so hard her shoulders nearly smacked her ears. 'Go ask him that.'

That's the problem. I can't ask him because I don't want to know the answer. Cold dread weighed her down. *Maybe he's leaving because he wants to get away.*

She didn't let her thoughts add the words 'from me' at the end of that sentence either.

'You're scared, aren't you?'

'Melody, stop reading my thoughts.' It was so annoying when her friend was right.

'I'm not, but it's pretty obvious what you're thinking. Ondi, you're going to have to ask him why he's leaving. If you do, you'll know why. If you don't, you never will.'

A heavy and overly dramatic sigh worked its way out of Ondine. 'You're right.'

The toothiest grin split Melody's face. 'Course I am. Anyway, your dreams aren't the only ones I visit.'

'No! You don't go into Hamish's dreams, do you?'

'I know he dreams about you.' Melody smiled even
more, then seemed to realise how inappropriate it was
and had the grace to look chastened.

'That's a terrible invasion of privacy!' Ondine
grinned. 'What were they about?'

Ping! went the microwave.

'Your milk's ready.' Melody fidgeted for a bit. 'Why
don't you take it to Hamish? I think he's having trouble
sleeping tonight as well.'

It was a good idea. All the excitement of the night
would make it hard for anyone to sleep. Taking him a
cup of warm milk would make her appear thoughtful
and considerate of Hamish's situation. And if anyone
saw her near his room and asked her what she was
doing there, she'd have a believable excuse.

'Thanks, Mel. Now, no more sneaking into people's
dreams.' Ondine made for the door, then wondered
which way to turn. The ferret Shambles might be
somewhere cosy, but where would the man Hamish be?

'Your ma's got him sharing a room with Thomas
and Chef down the hall in number thirteen,' Mel said
without needing to be asked.

'Thanks.' Stepping quietly so she didn't wake anyone else, Ondine made her way to room thirteen. Another problem stacked on to the already teetering tower of problems – how would she speak to him in private if Chef and Thomas were in there as well?

Or worse. What if the three of them were sound asleep and she woke the wrong person in the dark?

She stood outside room thirteen for a good minute, working out whether she should knock or just try and open the door as quietly as she could.

'What are you doing here?'

Gulp! It was Cybelle walking towards her. 'I just . . . I need to speak to –'

'Get back to bed or I'll tell Ma you were down here,' Cybelle said.

Great, so her sister was still cross with her. 'I'll tell her you were down here too. Then we'll both be in the same amount of trouble.'

'Except you're still grounded, so you'll be worse off.'

Gulp! She's right!

They were so busy trading quips Ondine didn't notice the door open. 'Evening, ladies.' Hamish stood there, wearing Da's old pyjamas and the wickedest grin she'd ever seen. It made her insides go all melty.

'*Kh.*' Cybelle made a disparaging sound. 'You two are hopeless. Is Henrik in there?'

'Aye.' Hamish may have been answering Cybelle as he stepped aside to let her through the door, but he kept his eyes firmly on Ondine.

Melty, melty, melty.

'I, um.' *Why is this so hard?* 'I couldn't sleep.'

'Can't blame ye really. Neither can I.'

'I have hot milk.' She held up her cup to show him.

Hamish beamed. 'Yer a thoughtful lass.' He tilted his head, indicating they should take a walk up the hallway to the lounge.

Miracle! Ondine's legs worked and she followed him. As they neared the private room by the kitchen, Hamish stepped back and whispered, 'This one's taken.'

Ondine craned her neck. 'Oh.' Marguerite and Thomas were talking quietly in there.

'The garden?' Hamish said with a shrug.

Still holding her cup of milk, Ondine followed him to the garden. The balmy summer night wafted the

285

scent of evening jasmine around them.

'This looks like a good spot,' Hamish said.

How sweet that he chose the same place where they'd shared That Beautiful Kiss. There was another part of the garden she didn't care for, where Lord Vincent had been such a pig. As if reading her thoughts, Hamish guided Ondine to sit with her back to the offending place so she wouldn't have to look at it. He took the cup of milk from her hand and placed it on the ground, then held her hands in his. Warmth spread through her at his touch.

The lovely surroundings should have given the ensuing conversation a dreamlike quality, but when she spoke, it all came out in a rush. 'Please don't go and work for the Duke.'

Seconds passed. All he did was look at her in that way of his and her heart felt like it was breaking against her ribs.

'Why not?'

'Because . . . because you don't have to. I'm sure Da would give you a job here if you asked him.'

'And take advantage of his hospitality? Nah. I've done that long enough.'

'But you're good. I mean, you won the tips competition easily. You charm the customers and everyone.'

'I appreciate the vote of confidence, but working for the Duke would be a great opportunity for me. Surely ye see that?'

'Yes, but . . .' Things twisted inside her, and it hurt to breathe. In her head, she played out a few scenarios.

Things in her favour – the darkness and the fact that Hamish would be leaving.

Things not in her favour – the darkness and the fact that Hamish would be leaving.

If she told him she loved him, and he stayed, it would be wonderful. If she told him she loved him and he left anyway, she'd die from a broken heart.

But if she didn't tell him she loved him, he would definitely leave. She didn't even want to think about what she'd tell her school friends when the new term began. They'd ask about how she spent her summer holidays and she'd burst into tears.

Heat raced up her neck. 'Hamish . . . I . . . I think I love you.'

Hamish leant forward and pressed his warm lips against hers, sending flurries through her. That bashing sound in her head was her pulse roaring into life. When he pulled away, her eyes were still closed.

'Ondine, I love you right back.'

'Oh, Hamish!' She threw her arms around his neck and hugged him. *What bliss, everything was going to be OK after all.*

'But I have to leave.'

'*What? No!*' With a thud Ondine fell back into her seat and stared at him. This was not going the right way! 'That's not how it works! I just bared my *soul* to you. I've never done that *ever*, and you say you're leaving *anyway*?'

'Aye.' He tucked a stray hair behind her ear and caressed her cheek with his palm. 'But knowing ye love me makes it easier. Gives me something to look forward to when I get back.'

'But . . . you don't need to leave in the first place. I know it's treason to say this,' she lowered her voice on the off-chance someone might overhear, 'but I've gone right off the Duke. I don't like the sort of job he's offering you.'

'What's nawt to like? I get to ferret around and make sure no trinkets end up in the wrong people's pockets.'

'It just doesn't *sound* right, that's why. He's a Duke. He's loaded. Why doesn't he install security cameras instead?'

Hamish cupped Ondine's cheek again. 'It's nawt really about the job description, is it? More the fact I'll be away that's upsetten ye.'

'I suppose so.' His warm hand felt so good she almost forgot her own mind.

'Ondi, I do love ye. Taking a job with the Duke is the perfect way for me to show ye how much.'

'What?' It made no sense at all. He loved her so he was leaving?

'Hear me out. It's been a long time since I was a real man. I want to get it right. That means being responsible. Getting a real job. Staying here, by the grace and favour of yer parents . . . that's nawt being responsible. Taking a real job with the Duke of Brugel will prove to yer parents that I'm worthy of ye. I'll be a man for the first time in me life.'

'But . . . the Duke wants you to be a *ferret*.'

'Aye, Ondi, we all have to make sacrifices.'

Heat burned the back of her eyes. Her vision blurred and a hot tear splashed down her cheek.

Jupiter's moons, now I'm crying like a nine-year-old.

'Ach, dry yer eyes. I'll nawt leave tomorrow. He doesn't need me until September. We've still got the rest of the summer, and then I'll only be across town. I'll come and visit whenever I can.'

'Promise?'

'Promise.'

Ondine threw her arms around Hamish and hugged him tightly. The thought of having to separate shredded her heart, so she wound her arms that bit tighter round him.

In the east, the faint glow of dawn broke the murky night sky.

'It's morning already,' Hamish said, noticing the change in the light.

'Maybe we should get inside?' An uneasy little flip began to flop inside Ondine's belly. Last time they'd been here in the garden, as dawn had broken, Hamish had reverted to ferret form.

'No. Let's see what happens.' Hamish cupped her chin, pulled Ondine closer and kissed her again, making her brain fizz and crackle. Every time their lips met her mind went all fuzzy and she loved it. She loved him. Even better, he loved her.

They pulled apart for a little bit, and checked the sky.

So far so good.

The sun cleared the horizon, bathing the air with the warming rays and colours of a new summer's day.

'You're still you,' Ondine beamed.

'Aye. See, being responsible is paying off already.'

'Good. Kiss me again then.'

He did as he was told and her whole body buzzed with the joy of it.

'Hamish? Promise me when you're working for the Duke that you'll come back as often as you can?'

'As long as ye promise to welcome me back like this each time.'

Ondine beamed. 'That's a very easy promise to make.'

As they kissed into the morning, Ondine banished thoughts of how soon autumn would be upon them. Instead, she focused on the precious few weeks of summer remaining, and the promises they'd made to each other.

Especially her promise about welcoming him back.

ACKNOWLEDGEMENTS

Thank you, Mum, for helping me grow. (I've found you a really nice nursing home . . . just kidding!)

Thank you to my husband for the constant support and suggestions. Some of them even made it into the book.

Thanks to my incredible agent Suzy Jenvey at PFD and my wonderful editors at Egmont, Leah Thaxton and Rachel Boden, for joining me on this strange journey through Brugel.